MODERN

Glamour. Power. Passion.

MILLS & BOON

First Published 2026
First Australian Paperback Edition 2026
ISBN 978 1 038 97447 1

MIX
Paper | Supporting responsible forestry
FSC® C001695

Published by
Harlequin Mills & Boon
An imprint of Harlequin Enterprises (Australia) Pty Limited
(ABN 47 001 180 918), a subsidiary of HarperCollins
Publishers Australia Pty Limited
(ABN 36 009 913 517)
Level 19, 201 Elizabeth Street
SYDNEY NSW 2000 AUSTRALIA

Printed and bound in Australia by McPherson's Printing Group

His Forced Sicilian Bride

Jackie Ashenden

MILLS & BOON

Books by Jackie Ashenden

Harlequin Modern

Spanish Marriage Solution
Newlywed Enemies
King, Enemy, Husband

The Teras Wedding Challenge

Enemies at the Greek Altar

Scandalous Heirs

Italian Baby Shock
The Twins That Bind

Work Wives to Billionaires' Wives

Boss's Heir Demand

Captured and Claimed

Christmas Eve Ultimatum
His Heir of Revenge

Visit the Author Profile page
at millsandboon.com.au for more titles.

Jackie Ashenden writes dark, emotional stories with alpha heroes who've just gotten the world to their liking only to have it blown apart by their kick-ass heroines. She lives in Auckland, New Zealand, with her husband, the inimitable Dr. Jax, two kids and two rats. When she's not torturing alpha males and their gutsy heroines, she can be found drinking chocolate martinis, reading anything she can lay her hands on, wasting time on social media or being forced to go mountain biking with her husband. To keep up-to-date with Jackie's new releases and other news, sign up to her newsletter at jackieashenden.com.

To my Oregon family (and that little trailer in particular).
Love you guys. <3

CHAPTER ONE

Caterina

I CLUTCH MY bouquet of calla lilies in sweaty hands, my stomach in knots. I'm in full bridal meringue, standing before the altar in a flouncy strapless gown of white silk, with a long gauzy veil held in place by a jewelled diadem. My father was grudging, saying at least I look the part, not that I care what he thinks.

Myself, I hate it. I hate all of it. I've never been the good, quiet Salvatore princess he wanted me to be. I'm too argumentative, too hot-tempered, too impulsive, and I hate being told what to do, all of which are terrible flaws in a daughter, according to my father.

But today is my wedding day and I have a part to play, no matter how much I hate it. As my father has impressed on me many times, I have to make up for the deaths of my mother and brother somehow, and all of this is for the good of the family.

The Roman cathedral where the marriage is taking place is full of people. My own family, the Salvatores, but also the families of our allies and naturally the family of my groom, Carlo Bianchi.

Our union was arranged years ago, by my father and Carlo's, while I was still under-age, and for the longest time I forgot I was Dad's most valuable pawn in his games of power. I was too busy completing my history degree via an online university and thinking about getting a job.

But naturally my father had other ideas. It was time I was married, he told me. Our hated enemy, the Wolf of Sicily, aka Vincenzo Argenti, head of the Argenti family, was growing ever more powerful and if we wanted to survive we had to ally with as many other families as we could. Marriage being the best way to do that.

I've got nothing against my groom, Carlo, but I barely know him and I suspect he feels the same about me. We both have no choice, though. In our families, in the *cosa nostra*, duty comes first and refusal is not an option. This is the way it's always been and my personal feelings about it matter not at all.

Behind me, in the pews, I hear people shuffle and whisper then quieten. My stomach tightens as the priest looks at me. He can probably see how white I am behind my veil, but there's nothing he can do for me. There's nothing anyone can do for me. My family, the Salvatores, were powerful once, but years ago, when I was a child, my mother and older brother were killed in an Argenti hit that left my father badly injured. It was a blow against our family that we've been trying to recover from ever since, and consequently that meant finding allies however and wherever we could. Being seen to be weak is not something we can afford, not if we want to survive.

I did try to get out of the marriage. In fact, I've spent the last month arguing with Dad about the necessity of it, but he insisted. The old ways of bonding allies, by blood, were the strongest and I would do this for the family whether I liked it or not. Dad's not big on choices.

Going against the head of the family isn't done, especially if you're a woman and the only child left. And most especially when your father has impressed upon you that if you don't do this, the deaths of your mother and brother would have been for nothing.

The priest intones the beginning of the ceremony and I feel the combined attention of thousands of eyes on me. A family wedding is always a big deal.

Carlo shifts on his feet—he's as excited as I am about this marriage, which is not at all—but he, at least, is present in the moment. I, on the other hand, am mourning the ending of my freedom, since once I'm his wife, I'll be his property. I'll be denied a career. My only value is my name and the protection it brings the Bianchis. Oh yes, I'll also be an acceptable vessel for children, because how else to breed the next generation of family soldiers?

This was never the life I wanted—I wanted to study more, and maybe teach or get a job in a museum—but it's the life I was born into and I have no choice. The silver lining is that at least as Carlo's wife I'll be out of my father's house in Rome, where I'm guarded and protected like a princess out of a fairy tale. Being the sole remaining child of a family is dangerous, since my destruction would also ensure the destruction of the Salvatore family.

Another reason I can't refuse my duty. I can't be responsible for the death of the Salvatores, that's a burden too heavy to bear, especially when I'm already carrying the deaths of my mother and brother. All I can do is marry Carlo and hope against hope that he'll allow me some semblance of freedom, at least as much freedom as the wife of one of the *cosa nostra* families can have. Ha.

I stare down at my feet in my white wedding slippers, trying to calm the frantic beat of my heart. It'll be okay, I tell myself. Being married to Carlo won't be so bad. It'll make my father happy, ensure our family's survival, and if I'm lucky, I'll be able to build some kind of life for myself that isn't just shopping and lunching, minding children and drinking cocktails with the other wives. I mean, really, it could be worse.

Except no matter how many times I tell myself that, I know it won't be okay, and the dread sits heavy and cold in my gut. Shopping and drinking cocktails is all very well, but the risk of death is ever-present. You'll always be a target and so will your children, and that's not the kind of life I want for either myself or any kids I have. To be always looking over your shoulder in case of car bombs or ambushes, or any one of the thousands of ways you can die.

I'm in the middle of these depressing thoughts and spiralling, when I hear more shuffling and whispering behind me. The priest is still speaking but gradually he slows down and stops, a frown appearing on his face.

I glance at Carlo, who is also looking over his shoulder and frowning, so I do too, turning to see what or who is creating all the fuss. And just as I do, the big double doors of the cathedral burst open and suddenly the entire nave is full of men carrying guns.

Chaos erupts. There are screams and shouts, people leaping up from the pews and calling for bodyguards, weapons being drawn, but a man is striding down the aisle. He's dressed in black, moving with a panther's grace, an apex predator in a room full of prey.

Everything about him is dark, including the wave of violent energy that seems to emanate from him. He's very tall, with black hair and sharp, sculpted features. Ink-black brows. A hard jaw. And eyes that burn like molten silver.

Those eyes are looking nowhere except straight at me.

I freeze, rooted to the spot as a wave of pure fear washes through me.

I know him. Everyone in the entire room knows him. It's the Sicilian Wolf himself, Vincenzo Argenti, and he's been slowly but surely amassing power and collecting allies for years. I've overheard Dad say that the Wolf wants all the families under his thumb and he'll stop at nothing to do that, though no one knows the truth for sure.

What is true that is that anyone who resists him ends up dead.

He's also the man who murdered my mother, Claudia, and my brother, Alessio.

'Nobody move,' the Sicilian Wolf says to the cathedral at large, his dark, deep voice echoing in the vaulted space. 'No one wants a bloodbath in a church. Though I assure you, if anyone lifts so much as a finger, I will not hesitate to start one.'

His men are everywhere, standing sentinel around the walls, semi-automatics pointed at the gathered wedding guests. I have no idea how they managed to get past the heavy security my father personally oversaw, but they have. Then again, I've heard all the stories about Vincenzo Argenti, how he can walk through walls and turn invisible at will, so who knows? Perhaps he and his men did exactly that.

A deafening silence has fallen as he strolls calmly towards me, ignoring Carlo, the priest and the rest of the gathered guests as if they don't exist.

'Caterina Salvatore,' he drawls, my name rolling off his tongue like fine wine. There's a rough timbre to his voice and a chill that ices my blood. 'A pretty name. But I think Caterina Argenti is even prettier.'

Caterina Argenti? What is he even talking about?

My thoughts reel about drunkenly then reality slowly adjusts itself. Vincenzo Argenti, the demon in the dark from the night Mama and Alessio died, is here, at my wedding. I remember him. He was with all the men with guns who came into our house, and he shoved me into a closet and locked the door. Then I heard the gunshots outside that killed my family. I was five.

To this day I don't know why he didn't kill me along with Mama and Alessio, but I was shut in that closet for a long time until someone found me. For years afterwards, I used to have nightmares about that closet, about him, and now he's here, holding up my wedding at gunpoint. Is he back to finish the job? To wipe out the Salvatores once and for all? Gun me down in front of the altar and then kill all the guests too?

Beside me Carlos makes a soft sound, then backs away rapidly. The priest begins to say something, but the Wolf lifts one long-fingered, commanding hand and the priest decides not to say something after all.

My bouquet of calla lilies falls out of my nerveless fingers and onto the stone floor, scattering petals everywhere.

The Wolf doesn't hesitate, walking straight up to me. Then he extends a hand. 'Shall we?' His silver eyes glitter and even the dusting of white at his temples doesn't detract from the impact of his physical presence. He's more frightening than anyone I have ever met, and I want to close my eyes, shut him out of my field of vision, pretend he's not there.

But he is there. He most definitely is.

'To be clear,' he goes on, steel in the words. 'That was not a request. That was an order.'

I'm too shocked to move, but this is happening, and slowly it penetrates what exactly 'this' is. His men are merely standing guard, not firing into the crowd, and he himself looks to be unarmed. He's certainly not pointing a weapon in my direction. Which means…

It's not a hit. It's a kidnapping. And he's kidnapping me.

When I don't move immediately, he makes a gesture and abruptly two gunmen appear beside me as Carlo and the priest back frantically away. My father is on his feet and so are his allies and they're all beginning to shout.

'Silence!' the Wolf thunders and a deathly quiet falls in the cathedral. He's still looking directly at me.

And deep down inside me, a small flicker of anger ignites.

I already didn't want to be here, and now the man of my nightmares is standing right there, making this terrible day even more terrible, and ordering me to do his bidding at gunpoint.

I've been ordered around by men my entire life and right now, right here, is the last straw. I'm tired of it. I'm tired of being my father's pawn in his relentless quest for allies. I'm tired of having my duty explained to me every goddamn day. I'm tired of having the deaths of Mama and Alessio flung in my face and used to manipulate me.

Tired of never having choices of my own.

So I don't move, merely lifting my chin instead, because at this point, I have nothing left to lose. 'So you're kidnapping me? Is that it?'

'You catch on quick.'

'Well,' I say, scraping together the dregs of my courage and lifting my chin even higher. 'Respectfully, I decline.'

His eyes glitter, and one side of his cruel mouth

curves. 'Respectfully or otherwise, your consent is not required.' He lifts his hand again and the man beside me shoulders his gun, puts his hands on my waist.

I tense, cold with fear but unwilling to let the Wolf see that. 'I see,' I say, forcing as much disdain as I can into my voice. 'Not strong enough to lift me yourself? Or are you not man enough? Which is it?' Either way, I'm going to be some man's property, so I might as well make it as hard for this particular man as possible.

Vincenzo Argenti's smile doesn't waver, but something leaps in his sharp silver eyes and it looks like amusement. 'Interesting,' he murmurs. 'Well, I've never been one to resist a challenge.'

Then before I can move, he motions his soldier aside, puts his own hands on my waist, before hauling me up and over his shoulder. Then he turns around and stalks out of the church, with me screaming obscenities in his ear.

CHAPTER TWO

Vincenzo

SHE'S A FIRECRACKER, I'll give her that, squirming and wriggling about on my shoulder while she screams in my ear. I have to tighten my grip on her to stop her from falling, which would very much ruin the performance I've just given back there in the cathedral.

Kidnapping isn't normally something I take a personal hand in—I leave that to my men—but this one was a special case and it required my presence.

I timed it perfectly, even if I do say so myself. I entered just as the ceremony was starting and everyone's attention was on the bride and groom. With the crowd distracted and the Salvatores' security poor, it was comparatively easy to get into the cathedral, though I have to admit that I didn't intend to put hands on Caterina Salvatore myself.

She stood at the altar, very tall and straight in a strapless, ivory silk gown that billowed around her like a cloud. Her long black hair had been piled on top her head in complicated curls, with a jewelled tiara crowning her, green eyes glinting at me from behind the silk of her veil.

The little girl I remembered from all those years ago was now a woman, and one who held herself like an empress.

I was expecting her to scream or at least to cower as I strode down the aisle towards her, yet she did neither. She was, in fact, furious, which I hadn't anticipated, since her wedding was one of necessity, or so my intel had informed me. Yet there was no denying the glitter of rage in her eyes, which made me wonder if she actually had feelings for the Bianchi boy.

Not that it matters. I would have taken her even if she was madly in love with him.

Still, it's interesting that he was the one cowering before me in fear, not her. No, she basically flung my lack of manhood in my face, and while I'm very much secure in that manhood, the one thing I can't resist is a challenge from a pretty woman. It added to the theatre of the moment, so I wasn't averse to flinging her over my shoulder—except I'm regretting that now as she screams curses in my ear. Clearly she didn't expect me to take her up on that challenge.

I stride down the steps to the waiting car, deafened by her continued shouting. She's certainly not the good, quiet Salvatore princess I was led to expect by my sources, nor does she bear much of a resemblance to the terrified little girl I shoved in a closet all those years ago. No, she's more a wildcat not wanting to be caught, which is unfortunate since I've now caught her.

By the end of the day, she'll be my wife and then

I'll have the perfect hostage to the Salvatores' good behaviour and that of their allies.

After my mother, Elena, died in a car bomb set by Salvatore soldiers, my father, Stefano, wanted the entire Salvatore family dead in revenge. But he failed. Now he's gone and I'm head of the family, my goal is to get rid of them in a different way. By marrying their last heir and making her an Argenti.

The Salvatores and their friends are the last holdouts, the last few families I have yet to bring under my control, and once Caterina is wearing my ring, they'll at last be brought to heel, making the Argenti clan the most powerful of the *cosa nostra* families in Sicily and Italy, if not all of Europe.

I have a reason for that, naturally enough, and it's not just about power. It's about the stain on the Argenti family honour, the stain put there by my father and his brutal killings of innocents. A stain I partially erased when I took him down myself, but there's more still to do. It's not enough that he's dead. I have to change things completely, end the violence. Unite the families, stop the feuding and the vendettas, stop the killings of family by family, and to do that I need them brought under my rule.

Whether they want to be there or not.

I'm tired of the constant march of death and violence, and I will not have it, even if I have to perpetuate a little death and violence myself. The end will ultimately justify the means.

Though, ironically, it was the death of my mother

and the Salvatores themselves that began this crusade of mine.

I was my father's good little soldier back then, and when he ordered me to take some men and hit the Salvatore family, avenge my mother's death and the stain on our family's honour, I obeyed without question.

She'd once been bright and beautiful, a loving mother to me, but over the years, marriage to my father drained the life out of her, turned her into a husk of the woman she'd once been. A woman who preferred lying in a darkened bedroom with her pills to being with me. Even so, her death was a shock and I was desperate to make someone suffer for her loss.

Yet once I got to the Salvatores' villa, everything changed.

Giovanni Salvatore must have had a warning that we were coming, because he was in the middle of escaping when we arrived. I got a shot at him, but it wasn't a kill shot, and he unfortunately got away. Some of my men went after him, while I took the rest into the villa to get rid of any remaining Salvatores.

The men took the downstairs, while I went upstairs, and that's when I found her. A little girl of no more than five. The Salvatore daughter, Caterina.

I was young, only twenty, yet already battle-hardened. Already wrought into the hard-line successor my father wanted and needed me to be, and I didn't expect this to be a hard task—I'd killed men before, after all.

But this wasn't a man, this was a child, and a child, it turned out, was different. She'd had a doll in her hand and the biggest green eyes I'd ever seen, her long black hair in braids. And she was terrified of me. Up until that point in my life, my father had taught me to have no morals and no boundaries except obedience to his will. Yet looking into the little girl's terrified eyes, I found I did, in fact, have morals and boundaries.

I could not kill a child. She was blameless, an innocent, and while my mother had been innocent and blameless, too, killing this girl wasn't going to bring her back. Even at twenty I didn't have much of a soul left, not after my father took over my upbringing. Still, I had enough of one to understand that if I killed this girl, there would be no going back, not for me. I would become my father entirely. It was in that moment I knew that I didn't want to be. I didn't *ever* want to be a man who put his own revenge above a child's life.

So I shoved her into a closet, ordered her not to make a sound, then I locked the door.

I went back downstairs, fully intending to stop the killing of Claudia and her son Alessio, my father be damned, but by the time I got down there, the rest of my men had already carried out my father's plan. Both were dead.

Stefano punished me for my 'failure' and I still bear the scars, but even so, it was then that I'd decided. Those scars would serve as my vow to end the killing of innocents. End the violence of family against family.

Caterina Salvatore was the catalyst for that vow, and it's fate that delivers her into my hands now. She's the last piece I need to bring the families into line and once that is done the jigsaw will finally be complete. The families united under one law: mine.

Satisfaction settles in me, the way it always does when a plan goes completely to my design, though it would have been more ideal had she not been screeching in my ear like a banshee. To make matters even more uncomfortable, I can feel the softness and heat of her body draped over my shoulder, the warm scent of jasmine releasing as she struggles.

I've always liked the smell of flowers, yet it's disturbing how much I like hers, mixed as it is with a musky, feminine note uniquely her own. I almost regret making her my wife in name only, but it's merely a passing thought and not enough to change my mind. I have no patience for seduction these days, let alone seducing a woman I once rescued as a child and who sees me as the enemy. It's not as if I don't have many lovers anyway.

She lands yet another fist on my back as I approach the car, striking me as if she has no conception of who I am and what happened to the last person who laid a hand on me in anger. What she should be is grateful that I decided on marriage as the way to bring the Salvatores and their allies to me, instead of gunning everyone in that cathedral down. That's what my father would have done. My *consiglieri* was doubtful of the plan, since leaving anyone alive is not without its risks, but I wanted to do it without bloodshed.

Dio, I'm in danger of fucking growing a halo.

My driver has the door open for me and as I'm stuffing the wildcat inside, she manages to land a glancing blow to my temple with one flailing hand. My driver goes for his gun, but I shake my head and wave him away. She's no threat to me, lucky blow or otherwise.

She inhales sharply as I shove her into the seat then jerk the seat belt across her, buckling her up even as she tenses, ready for another round. Safety first for my future wife.

'You were a lot less trouble when you were five, *gattina,'* I tell her.

'Bastard,' she spits as the car pulls away from the kerb, the rest of my men following in other cars behind us. 'I'm not a little cat. And you didn't need to throw me over your shoulder like a sack of bloody potatoes! I would have come quietly.'

'Would you?' I give my temple a theatrical rub. 'I've killed men for less than that blow you just gave me.'

She glances at my forehead then back at me, not an ounce of contrition in her emerald gaze. 'Kill me then. I should have hit you harder.'

'My,' I murmur, amused by her fire. 'So bloodthirsty.' And it's strangely refreshing. I can't remember the last time a woman was so furious with me, or at least not so openly. People tend to tread lightly whenever I'm around.

I sit back in my seat and take a moment to study her.

She's radiating anger, glowering at me like I'm not the most feared man in all of Europe, though I suspect that beneath that fury, she's afraid. But she's not giving in to it and that takes a certain amount of courage.

Interesting. It seems my bride-to-be is a little warrior, though she doesn't look like one, dressed as she is in a flamboyant white wedding gown and veil. Her tiara is slightly askew and some of her glossy black hair has come out of its pins, and her pale skin is flushed with temper.

The little girl I protected has blossomed into a very pretty woman, it seems. Not that I require her to be pretty or indeed anything other than being a Salvatore. Her name and her value as a hostage are the most important things.

'I could in fact kill you,' I say. 'Would you like that?'

'That's why you took me, isn't it?' Her pointed chin lifts, her expression half defiant, half imperious. 'So you could finish the job you started twenty years ago?'

So, the little *gattina* remembers me. I wasn't sure if she did.

'If I wanted to do that, you'd be dead already,' I observe. 'But you were right back there in the cathedral.'

Her long, thick black lashes flutter as she blinks rapidly. 'You kidnapping me, you mean? Oh…' Understanding dawns. 'I'm a hostage.'

I give her a slow smile, because I do like an intelligent woman. 'Excellent answer. Ten points to you.'

'My father will—'

'Your father,' I interrupt, 'is irrelevant, no matter what he will or won't do. I'm afraid, *gattina*, no one is going to save you this time.'

The delicate bow of her mouth, highlighted by some kind of shimmery pink lipstick, compresses into a line and fear flickers briefly in her eyes.

I expect her to cower in her seat, but she doesn't.

Instead, she stares back at me, undaunted despite her fear. ‘So? I’m going to be your prisoner?’

‘No, *gattina,*’ I correct her gently. ‘You’re going to be my wife.’

CHAPTER THREE

Caterina

THE AIR IN the car feels as if all the oxygen has been replaced by something else, something sparking and electric and tense. I'm already breathless from being thrown over this despicable man's shoulder and carried ignominiously from the cathedral—admittedly, I have only myself to blame for that—but what he's said just now has taken away what little breath I have left.

His wife? His *wife?*

He's leaning back in his seat as if he's at home, lounging in a favourite chair, one foot propped on the opposite knee, his large, long-fingered hands loose on his thighs. He's overwhelming close up, his kinetic, violent presence filling the car, while his intense silver gaze burns into me.

The man of my nightmares is right here and not only has he taken me hostage, now he's telling me he's going to make me his wife.

I almost can't take it in.

'It's a shock, I know,' he says, his voice deep and lazy, a thread of dark amusement winding through it.

'Luckily though, you're already dressed for the occasion.'

'I'm not marrying you,' I say, my temper running away with my tongue before I can stop myself. 'You can take your damn proposal and shove it up your arse.'

The smile that plays around his mouth makes it curve into something like a sneer, while his eyes glitter like diamonds, hard and sharp. 'Such language,' he murmurs, chiding. 'Also, you're incorrect. I did not propose. I merely told you what is going to happen irrespective of where you wish to shove it.'

His measured response is disconcerting. I'm expecting him to be angry, because every man in the families gets angry when a woman talks back. We're expected to be pretty and decorative, to have no opinions except about child-rearing, household management, cocktails and shopping. And we're definitely not allowed to swear. My father would have had fifty fits listening to me shout the moment Vincenzo Argenti flung me over his shoulder.

I really *wasn't* expecting him to do that, no matter how stoutly I dared him to, so I got the shock of my life when he picked me up as if I weighed nothing. Then shock was replaced by fury. The ignominy of being carried out of my own wedding like a naughty child was too much, and yes, I lost my temper. It's never too far from the surface, no matter how hard I try to push it down, and it overcame my fear, spilling out inside me like lava.

Not that hitting or shouting made any difference to the Wolf of Sicily.

His shoulder beneath my stomach felt like stone, his arm wrapped around my thighs an iron band. My fists on his strong back made no impact and I felt every bit of my powerlessness and fragility in that moment. He could have done whatever he wanted with me and I wouldn't have been able to do a single thing to stop him. Now, he wants to marry me and I can't stop him from doing that either.

I can't stop him from doing anything at all.

His manner is lazy, but I don't make the mistake of thinking he's anything but lethal, no matter how casually he lounges in the seat next to me.

'I won't do it,' I say, even though it doesn't matter and it's going to happen whether I want it to or not. 'I won't say "I do".'

'Yes, you will.' His head tilts, the afternoon sun glossing his black hair. 'Because if you don't, your father won't live to see another sunrise.'

I go cold. My issues with my father are many and varied, but even so, I don't want him to die. And I certainly don't want his death on my conscience, not when the deaths of Mama and Alessio weigh so heavily on me already.

I wish I could tell myself that this man wouldn't kill my father, but he would. Of course he would. Without a second thought. There's no mercy in those silver eyes, no kindness. No gentleness. I'll never know why he spared me all those years ago, but I don't want to know. These are the eyes of the killer who pushed me into a closet and locked the door, before walking away to murder the rest of my family.

'You can't force someone into marriage,' I shoot back, purely for form's sake, since I'm pretty sure he could force anyone into anything.

'I won't be forcing you, *gattina,*' he says as if my objections are of no moment. 'You'll be choosing to marry me to help your father stay alive.'

I stare daggers at him.

He merely smiles that cruel smile again and adds, 'It's a matter of perspective, you see?'

'You're a bastard,' I repeat, pointlessly.

'You should vary your insults. You've already called me a bastard more than once. Try something new, hmm?'

'Son of a bitch,' I growl through gritted teeth.

He lifts one straight black brow. 'Better. Though not very imaginative. Then again, I don't suppose imagination is encouraged in the Salvatore family.'

Insulting him is futile. Why bother?

Good question. I want to keep arguing with him, which is stupid, because it's not going to get me anywhere. Besides, my anger is just a mask for the fear that lies cold and sharp in my stomach. That fear makes me feel like that helpless little girl again, shoved into the darkness with the door shut in her face. Not being able to get out no matter how hard she kicked at the door, then hearing the gunshots…

I've had claustrophobia ever since and it's sliding its icy fingers around my throat and squeezing tight even now. I fight it though, because I'm not going to have a panic attack in front of this man. Nor am I going to lose my temper again. I need to put on the imperfect mask I managed to develop after my mother and brother died, when I was forced into the part of being a good Salvatore daughter. Where I had to keep my temper locked down and my tongue under control, or else risk punishment from my father.

The Wolf frowns, his focus on me intensifying in a way that makes me even more breathless than I already am. 'You look like you're about to have a panic attack,' he observes almost clinically. 'I have some sedatives if you need to take one.'

My temper rises at his tone, but I have myself under better control now. 'No, thank you,' I say stiffly. 'I prefer to experience my nightmares fully conscious.'

Again, the corner of his mouth lifts and I get the impression that once again I've amused him somehow. 'Don't worry, *gattina.* All I need from you is your physical presence at the ceremony and your name on the marriage certificate. I will not be needing you in my bed.'

For a second I can't process what he's saying, and then abruptly, I do. Sex. He's talking about sex. As soon as the thought occurs to me, I become suddenly and intensely aware of him. Of his powerful, physical presence in the car. Of how near he is to me, one hard muscled thigh brushing the white silk of my wedding gown. Of the way he's looking at me, both lazy and intense at the same time, those sharp silver eyes cutting right through me.

I've been protected all my life, guarded and warded

like Rapunzel in her tower. I went to a private girls' school, and when I went to university, it was online. I've never been alone with a man who wasn't either related to me, employed by my father, or been an ally of his. I've certainly never had a boyfriend.

That doesn't mean I don't know how sex works, though. I've seen things online and I know how to give myself pleasure. But I've never met a man I've been attracted to and this man, this nightmare of mine, sitting right next to me should be the last man on earth I'd ever feel the slightest pull of attraction towards.

But now he's mentioned his bed and me being in it, and now my brain is off and running, wondering what it would be like and I don't understand why I'm thinking about that. I don't understand why I'm blushing, either.

'Good,' I snap, pushing those thoughts away. 'Because even if you were the last man on earth I wouldn't sleep with you. I'd rather sleep with a goat.'

'Careful, *gattina,*' he says, amused again. 'I think you're in danger of liking me just a little.'

He's goading me and I know it. But I'm also aware that there's a piece of me, way down deep inside, that is almost…enjoying this. Because for a long time I've struggled with who my father wanted me to be and who I actually am. At first all I wanted was to be his good, obedient girl. I wanted him to notice me, be proud of me, be glad that I hadn't died along with Mama and Alessio.

But no matter how hard I tried to be good, he wasn't proud and he wasn't glad, and when he drank too much at night sometimes, he'd tell me that he wished I'd died instead of Alessio, because then he'd still have an heir.

It hurt. It hurt to know that nothing I did or would ever do, would be enough for him. And the worst part of all was the fact that he was my father and I still loved him.

But I don't love Vincenzo Argenti or care about his feelings, and so there's a bit of me that doesn't want to keep the mask on. A bit of me that wants to argue and shout, and unleash myself on him. Cut the man of my nightmares down to size, because he is, after all, just a man, even if he is the head of the most powerful clan in Europe.

'Oh sure,' I say, my tone dripping with sarcasm. 'Yes, of course I'm in danger of liking the man who killed my family.' I grit my teeth as I hold his gaze, grasping on to my rage for courage. It's a mistake to keep snapping at him, because who knows what he might do? Still, I can't be more afraid than I am already and he said he wouldn't kill me.

The Wolf's brows twitch. 'Your father isn't dead.'

'No, but my mother and brother are.' My fingers curl in the silk of my gown, holding on tight as if I'm trying to stop myself from falling from a great height. 'I heard the gunshots after you shut me in the closet. You shot them both—'

'I did not shoot them,' he interrupts with some patience. 'They were both dead by the time I got downstairs.'

I blink. My father always told me that Vincenzo Argenti gunned them down in cold blood, and I had no reason to disbelieve him. But now he is saying he *wasn't* the one who killed them? 'Why should I believe a single thing you say?' I demand.

'You shouldn't. I don't care whether you believe me or not, but the truth is that I didn't kill your mother and brother, though I was ordered to.' His lazy silver gaze becomes somehow even sharper. 'I was ordered to kill you too.'

A small, cold shock goes through me, though I'm not sure why. I know he was there to kill me. I saw his eyes as he burst into my bedroom while I was playing with my doll. They were like ice, cold and dead. Even at five I knew I was in terrible danger, and I didn't need to see the gun in his hand to know that. Except he didn't shoot me. He shoved me into a closet and locked the door instead.

I've never wanted to know why he saved me. I was happy making him the monster, because it was easier to blame him than blame myself. But now, I'm almost compelled to ask, 'Why didn't you?'

He doesn't answer immediately, his gaze roving over me as if committing me to memory. It makes me uncomfortable, makes me want to shift in my seat, makes my skin feel tight. Makes me want to open the door and leap out onto the traffic, which is a bit over-dramatic, even for me.

Then he says, 'I suppose, since you're going to be my wife, you deserve some kind of explanation.'

I open my mouth to tell him that as the man who allegedly killed my family, I don't care what he thinks

I deserve or otherwise, but he holds up a peremptory hand. And much to my irritation, I fall silent.

'My father wanted revenge for the death of my mother. We had word the bomb that killed her was set by a Salvatore, and so he ordered the deaths of your family, and I was to carry it out.' The words are cool and there's a slight impatience to them, as if he's annoyed at having to explain. 'I shot your father, but that didn't take, alas. He escaped, so I went upstairs to find the rest of your family, but I only found you in your little pink bedroom.' His gaze is a steady burn of silver. 'You were holding a doll in one hand and all I could see were your big green eyes staring up at me. You must understand, *gattina,* up until that point, I was my father's man through and through. I burned for the revenge he wanted me to take and I was determined to get justice for my mother. But I saw you and… Well, let's just say I discovered a line I didn't know I had.'

I remember that night distinctly and the sight of his cold, dead eyes. 'A…line?' I ask.

'Yes. I found I didn't want to kill a child in revenge for my mother's death.' He's sitting very still, eyeing me like a bird of prey sighting a mouse in the grass. 'So, I shut you in the closet and locked the door so my men wouldn't find you. Then I went downstairs to stop them from killing your mother and brother, only to find that they were already dead.'

CHAPTER FOUR

Vincenzo

THOSE GREEN EYES of hers are wide and I can see shock in them, which is interesting. I don't know why I'm explaining myself to her, but I thought that since she *is* going to be my wife, she should know that her mother and brother didn't die by my hand. Clearly, her father has been feeding her all kinds of bullshit about what happened that night, so I'm happy to give her the truth. It's tedious to explain oneself, yet there's an unexpected pleasure to be had in upending her expectations about me.

I prefer people to be afraid, it makes them much more biddable, and over the years I've accepted that I'll always be the villain of the piece. That's the role I took on when I decided on my crusade, because the people I'm dealing with only understand one thing: violence.

But now I'm discovering that there's satisfaction in seeing the shock in her eyes. Shock that I'm *not* the villain she was expecting, or rather, less of the villain than she was expecting—I'm certainly not ever going to be the hero.

'Don't tell me,' I say, since she says nothing. 'Your father has been busy laying the deaths of your mother and brother at my feet for years.'

Her hands grip the white silk of her gown as if she wants to tear the fabric apart and for a second the image of me tearing apart the white silk myself to lay her bare flickers in front of my eyes. A kick of unexpected heat goes through me and I'm shifting in my seat before I can stop myself.

What the fuck? It's been years since I've experienced an unanticipated attraction, and I certainly don't want to experience one for Caterina Salvatore. She's pretty, yes, but she's too young and I'm a man of sophisticated appetites. I have lovers who satisfy me, who don't want more, so why I'm currently thinking about ripping her wedding gown off her, I have no idea.

Maybe I'll organise a wedding night after all, but with one of my current mistresses. Annika likes it rough and she's always ready for me.

'You were there, though,' Caterina says. Her voice has a trace of huskiness that I find more attractive than I care to admit. 'And you shot him.'

'I did,' I acknowledge. 'And I was. But the bullets that found your mother and brother did not come from my gun.'

'But…' She trails off, still staring at me.

I lift a brow. 'But what?'

'You just…didn't want to kill a child? That's the only reason you spared me?' She says this with some disbelief, and I don't blame her. Our world is a violent one, where innocents are hurt or killed all the time. Where fathers beat the shit out of their sons and mothers don't lift a finger to help. Having scruples is unusual.

'Yes,' I say dryly. 'Did you know that outside the families, that's actually considered a normal reaction?'

The flush in her cheeks deepens. Sparks of her ready temper glitter in her eyes. Clearly she didn't appreciate my sarcasm and she's still struggling with whether to believe me or not.

I don't care. Her belief or otherwise won't change what's going to happen.

She looks down at her hands for a moment, then abruptly back at me. 'Why do you need my family's good behaviour?'

'Finally,' I murmur. 'That should have been your first question.'

'Apologies. I was too busy screaming in terror when you carried me out of the cathedral to think about the right questions to ask.'

Oh, she's sharp, this one. I like it. I like it very much.

'You weren't screaming with terror, *gattina*.' I smile. 'You were screaming with rage.'

She scowls. 'Answer the damn question.'

No one speaks to me this way. My bodyguards would have a gun to her head if they were in the car with us right now and she should know that, having been brought up in the *cosa nostra*. I'm not offended, though. As I've already thought, she's no threat to me. Still, if she continues to push, she'll find I have a line and once she hits it, I'll push back. Hard.

'Ask me nicely,' I say lazily. 'And I might consider explaining myself.'

Her chin juts, gaze mutinous. 'Please.' She spits the word out like poison.

I'm entertained by her temper. 'Because I want them under my control, of course.'

'What for?'

'Demanding, *gattina.* You do realise that I am probably the most feared and powerful man in all the families, don't you?'

'I don't care what or who you are,' she snaps. 'I'm not asking for my freedom. All I'm asking for is a reason.'

Well, I certainly can't fault her courage. In fact, it makes me want to give her that reason and for free. Revealing one's plans, though, is a risk and one I never take if I can help it. Because once people discover what you're trying to do, they'll use that knowledge to stop you any way they can, and I know the families. Information is a precious commodity. If this one knows about my crusade, then she could pass that onto her father. Then again, as my wife she'll be under my complete control and I'm certainly not going to give her any opportunity to speak to her father or ever let her see him again. So, what could it hurt?

'The reason?' I echo. 'I'm bringing all the families under my control so the in-fighting and the feuds stop. So the killing of innocents stops.'

Her eyes widen. 'That's it? That's the reason?'

There's something about the way she says it that gets under my skin, as if she's shocked that I should want the violence to end. I understand why—my reputation isn't exactly snow-white—but she has no concept of what it is to be brought up as a family's heir. How, at twelve years old, my father forced me to attend the torture session of a suspected mole, and at fifteen, handed me a gun and made me shoot a family soldier who'd betrayed us. 'It's either you or him,' my father had said when I'd showed reluctance. 'And if you can't do it, I'll shoot you myself.'

'Yes,' I say, allowing a note of anger to show in my voice. 'Do you have a problem with that?'

She flushes and I find my gaze drawn to how the pink extends down her elegant throat and down below the neckline of her gown, where the fabric is pulled tight over a pair of small, high, beautifully shaped breasts.

'No,' she says quickly. 'No. I just...'

'Didn't expect the Sicilian Wolf to care about anyone's life?'

She looks away and once again I feel a wave of satisfaction that I've surprised her, which is puzzling.

Before I can interrogate the feeling though, my phone goes off and I answer it. There are a few logistical issues that need attention, so I spend the rest of the ride to my Roman villa, where the helipad is located, dealing with them.

Once we arrive at the villa, we go straight to the chopper and my wife-to-be says nothing as she is bundled into it. I have a few more business calls to make, so I spend the flight to Sicily making them and putting out the fires that my bride stealing has ignited. I order Elio, my *consiglieri*, to get Giovanni Salvatore's vow of loyalty to me by sundown in return for the life of his daughter, and then I double-check my security.

An hour or so later, we're coming down onto the rolling green lawn of the Argenti family villa. It's built on the clifftops overlooking the Aegean, with stone terraces descending amid cliffs and greenery, all the way down to the sea. A deep blue-green infinity pool reaches the edge of one terrace, shaded by olive trees and white outdoor umbrellas.

The villa itself is two storied and made of white-washed stone, surrounded by lawns and beautifully manicured gardens. It was my mother's pride and joy, and so I employ a couple of expert gardeners to keep it looking as she would have wanted it.

Caterina stares out the window as we land, her expression guarded. She didn't say a word on the way over and I find myself wondering what she thinks of the villa, though why I care I have no idea. I love the place myself, but my little crusade doesn't leave me with as much time to spend here as I'd like.

The helicopter touches down, my various staff all lined up, waiting for me to disembark so we can get the ceremony started immediately. The Argenti family priest, Father Giuseppe, is also waiting.

I open the door, get out, then extend a hand to Caterina. She glances at it, and with that same mutinous expression I saw in the car back in Rome, she ignores it and slips from the helicopter without help.

Stubborn *gattina*.

Again, I'm amused, though I will be less so if she's

going to be this stubborn during our marriage ceremony.

I stride over the grass to greet my staff and Father Giuseppe. Caterina follows me, looking around her warily.

'Come, *gattina.*' I indicate for her to stand beside me.

A ripple of shock crosses her face as she looks at me, then the priest, then back again. 'What?' Her voice has risen. 'You want to get married here? *Now?*'

'Of course. I kidnapped you already dressed for a reason.'

She's standing there as stiff as a post, her back rigid, yet there's something oddly commanding about her. Something proud. And a part of me, the darkness that lives inside me, the wolf, finds that impressive. That even though she's been kidnapped from her wedding by the man she thought killed her family, here she is, standing brave and strong rather than cowering in fear.

She will make an excellent Argenti wife.

The thought snakes through my head, despite having never given much thought as to what kind of wife I wanted. I knew I would marry one day, but I didn't want to do that until I'd consolidated my power base, and that has taken me longer than I thought it would.

So when I received intel that Caterina Salvatore would be marrying Carlo Bianchi in a bid to bolster Salvatore alliances, it was clear what I needed to do and quickly. Too quickly to think about what kind of wife she'd make for me.

But now I've been in her company a few hours, I'm

coming round to the idea that yes, she *would* make an excellent Argenti wife. She certainly has the force of will to be one.

She will make an excellent mother, too.

Oh yes, she will indeed. She's fiery and brave, at least what little I've seen of her has been, and those are excellent qualities in a mother. My own, for example, was both before my father's treatment of her crushed the life out of her. He'd wanted another child, but after three miscarriages, he lost patience with her and abandoned her here at the estate.

I won't do that to Caterina, though. I'll need heirs—someone has to carry on my legacy after I'm gone—but if we can't conceive naturally there's always adoption. I'm not as wedded to blood ties as my father was.

'Your father's life depends on your cooperation,' I remind her gently. 'It won't take long, I promise.'

She glares at me then moves, coming to stand beside me, regal as a queen. She very determinedly does not look at me and as the priest begins the ceremony, I find myself staring at her profile, noting the soft curve of her cheek and the lush fullness of her mouth. Her silky black brows and the slight tilt of her nose.

Pretty *gattina.*

When the time comes for her to face me and say her vows, she does so even though her whole body radiates negation and reluctance and fury. Her green eyes burn with rage, and her voice is full of venom as she spits the vows at me. With her tiara askew and her hair half down, she should look ridiculous, yet she doesn't. She looks like a murderous goddess, and I'm confounded by my growing interest in her.

When I planned this, I didn't think of her as a person—or at least, if I did, it was the five-year-old girl I was thinking of, not the woman. But it's the woman I'm marrying now and she's forcibly bringing me face-to-face with the fact that she's not a puzzle piece or a pawn. First with the screaming, then with her flailing hands. Then her quick-fire sarcasm and obvious fury.

She's intriguing, nothing like the women I bed who tend to fawn on me, or the wives of my men and those in other families, who smile sweetly and make no fuss, embracing their roles as adjuncts to their husbands.

You didn't want that kind of wife anyway.

No, I didn't.

She puts out her hand for a ring to put on my finger, but I don't have one for myself. The only ring I wear is my father's heavy gold signet with the Argenti crest, so I take that off and put it in her hand.

It looks huge in her small palm and when she looks up at me, I can see her battle the overwhelming urge to fling the ring in my face. I dare her to silently, but she only sniffs and pushes the ring back onto my finger.

Then it's my turn with the vows, and as I repeat the words, I can't help but reach out and adjust the tiara on her head, before pushing a strand of silky black hair back behind her ear. Her eyes widen as my fingertip brushes the tip of her ear, and she goes very still, electricity sparking between us at my touch.

The surprise of it jolts me, because while I enjoyed her scent and found her interesting, I hadn't planned on seducing a very clearly unwilling woman. But… perhaps she's not so unwilling after all?

Her lashes lower, hiding her gaze, yet it's too late. We were both caught off-guard by that spark of chemistry, and now we both know it's there. Or rather, *I* know it's there.

I was expecting to have an on-paper wife, while still seeing my usual lovers, but perhaps it's worth revising that decision. What would all that fire and fury look like turned into passion? Would she be as fierce in bed as she is out of it?

Something inside me shifts, a thread of desire winding tight, but it's not the time, so I push it aside, taking the ring out of my trouser pocket instead. Then I take her hand and slide it onto her finger as I repeat the vows. It's a simple band of white gold I bought on the way to the cathedral, but a stray thought tells me I should have had emeralds inlaid on it somewhere, to match her eyes.

Ridiculous. I buy jewels to match the eyes of my mistresses, not my wife.

'You may kiss the bride,' the priest says.

Caterina lifts her lashes and looks up at me, her green gaze silently challenging me the way I challenged her to throw my ring at my head.

I dare you to kiss me, she's saying, and not because she doesn't want it, she does. I can see it in her eyes, the curiosity and the heat. She wants to know if that spark between us was real or if she was imagining it, and I'm tempted to show her exactly how real it was.

But she's expecting me to do that, so instead I reach

out to cup her face between my palms. Then I bend my head, kiss her chastely on the forehead, before turning and striding into the house.

CHAPTER FIVE

Caterina

I STARE AT the Wolf's back as he disappears into the villa, my heart racing, and I don't know whether to be furious that he kissed me on the forehead like a child, or relieved.

No, I know. I'm relieved. I'm definitely very relieved. Because that would be my first kiss and there's no way I want that kiss to be from him. Ugh, the very thought of it…

You couldn't breathe at the very thought of it.

I ignore the voice in my head, because it's not true, absolutely not. Yet, I can't deny that when he lifted his long-fingered hands to adjust my tiara, and the tip of his finger brushed my ear as he pushed a lock of hair behind it, a bolt of electricity went through me. Part of me wanted to believe it was only static, but the rest of me knows that's not what it was. I saw the way his eyes flared. He felt that electricity, too.

And yes, as much as I don't want to admit it, when he cupped my face between his warm palms and I thought he was going to kiss me, I felt as if I might faint. All I could see was his silver gaze and the heat burning in the depths, and something hot in me stirring and waking up, wanting to play…

But I can't think about that. I don't want to. He's the enemy and the ring on my finger feels heavy, and I still can't believe that I'm here, at the Argenti villa in Sicily, married to the Sicilian Wolf.

On the helicopter ride over here, I tried thinking through plans on how I could escape or maybe get the information he told me about his intentions to my father, but none of them seemed viable. I don't have anything with me, not even my phone, and now I'm here at the Argenti villa, my options for escape or at least getting word to Dad, have narrowed considerably.

The late afternoon sun is beating down and the emotional fallout from the last couple of hours is catching up with me. I feel lost, cut adrift, alone in a forest of enemies with no one to turn to and nowhere to go, and married to a complete stranger.

As I'm standing there wondering what the hell to do next, a woman comes over to me and takes my arm, murmuring that she is Maria, the housekeeper, and she will take me to my room. I let her lead me into the villa, all the energy I had to fight with now gone.

Though my temper rouses slightly on the brief tour of the villa, mainly because it's beautiful, and I don't want to it to be beautiful, with its whitewashed walls and stone floors. Lots of light streams through tall windows with deep sills, silken carpets creating splashes of colour and softness. The furniture is very old, of dark wood, which contrasts with some of the abstract art on the walls.

Maria takes me upstairs and shows me into a beautiful room that faces the sea. The ivory linen curtains are pulled back from the windows while beneath them sits a squashy couch upholstered in faded pink velvet.

Against the opposite wall is a huge four-poster bed hung with white gauze, an antique dresser standing nearby. Bright cushions that carry the same pink as the couch are scattered on the seats and on the bed. Another silk carpet covers the stone floor, the same faded pink in amongst subtle hues of dusty blue and purple.

Maria gestures to the door on the other side of the room, which apparently leads to the en suite bathroom, and then at the sliding mirrored doors that hide a closet. The master has bought me everything I might need, or so she says, and I'm very tempted to ask if that includes a private plane to take me far away from here, because that's what I need most of all. But I keep my mouth shut. There's no point being rude to Maria. None of this is her fault.

Once she leaves me alone, I tear off my tiara and veil, and fling them on the bed. Then I claw at the fastenings of my stupid wedding gown. It feels as if it's suffocating me and I can't get it off fast enough. Beneath it I'm wearing a white silk strapless bra and white silk knickers, all lacy and transparent, because I thought Carlo would like them. But they, too, seem ridiculous now, so I claw them off as well until I'm wearing nothing except Vincenzo Argenti's ring.

I want to pull that off too, and hurl it into the sea,

but I have a feeling that he wouldn't care, which makes hurling it anywhere far less satisfying. In the end, I keep it on as I fling open the closet doors to see if he really did buy me everything I might need.

Looks like Maria wasn't wrong since it's full of newly bought clothes, all of them giving off major *cosa nostra* wife vibes. I ignore them and instead go to the dresser, pulling open all the drawers to see what else is in there. Sadly, at first glance, there are no practical underwear. It's all silk and lace, with tiny straps that look incredibly uncomfortable. I finally settle on a pair of purple silk knickers, with a sports bra I manage to unearth in the bottom drawer. There are also some loose black lounge pants in a soft, stretchy fabric that look comfy, so I put them on with an oversized sweatshirt in deep forest green.

They're familiar, these kinds of clothes. They're the opposite of dressed-up and put-together, which my father always wanted me to be since it showed me off as a trophy better, and once they're on, I feel less like a stolen bride, and more like myself.

On top of the dresser are pots and bottles of makeup, along with hairbrushes, eyelash curlers and all kinds of beauty products that I don't want or need. He's bought them for the wife he wants, not the woman I am, which is a familiar feeling, and so I ignore them all.

Instead, finding a black hair tie, I put my hair into a low ponytail so it's out of the way, then I go over to one of the French doors and open them so I can step out onto the terrace. The air is warm and scented with salt from the sea and rosemary from the pots that sit near the stone balustrade.

Below me I can see the green lawn roll to the edge of the cliffs and the deep blue of the Aegean beyond that. It's a beautiful view, but no amount of inhaling the scented air and gazing out at the ocean will change the fact that this villa is a prison, and I know it is because there are men in dark suits everywhere, patrolling the grounds. Argenti security no doubt.

The helicopter on the lawn takes off in a roar and a press of air, soaring up into the blue sky, and I wish I was on it. I wish I could fly away too, but I'm stuck down here, married to my family's hated enemy. Really, marrying Carlo would have been a walk in the park compared to this, because while we didn't know each other well, I didn't think he was all that bad. Certainly, I could have done worse.

You did do worse.

Anger wells up again at the thought, so I turn away from the beautiful view and the lie of freedom it represents, and go back into the bedroom. I try the bedroom door to see if it's locked, and I'm almost shocked to find that it isn't. I guess I shouldn't be surprised. It's not as if I can go anywhere given the level of security in the villa and grounds.

I open the door and step into the hallway outside. There's no one there, but a lovely stained glass window at one end casts colours on the stone floor.

Gathering my determination to at least check out the prison I find myself in, I spend time opening the doors on the top floor, finding more bedrooms, a couple of bathrooms and an elegant salon. Most of the bedrooms look as if they're not used frequently, which means they're probably for guests.

But there's one that *is* clearly in use, its door opposite mine in the hallway, and it's large, with another four-poster bed against one wall, an antique dresser against another. It's very plain, with no couch beneath the windows or silken carpet on the floor, but all the bottles on the dresser are arranged neatly, and everything is very tidy.

The room smells pleasantly of smoke and cedar, the scent sadly familiar. It smells of him, which means this must be *his* bedroom.

Vincenzo Argenti's bedroom.

I freeze in the doorway, listening for any noise, because I don't want to be found lurking creepily around. Yet I also don't want to leave. Maybe somewhere in here is a key or a phone or something I could use to get word to my father. Or maybe even to get out of the villa entirely.

Hearing nothing, I take a little breath and begin to explore.

On top of the dresser are various aftershave bottles, a hairbrush and comb, but nothing else. The drawers themselves reveal only clothes, and nothing much else of interest. After I've exhausted the dresser, I go over to the closet doors and slide them open, seeing only a line of perfectly tailored suits, all in various shades of grey, black and blue. Shirts, neatly pressed, hang next to them, all without exception either white or black.

Clearly, he doesn't like colour or mess, and it's very

irritating that there isn't anything immediately obvious lying around that I can use to escape with.

Turning from the closet, I go over to one of the bedside tables. There's nothing on top of it, but when I pull open the drawer I find boxes of condoms and, lying next to them, a gun.

A rush of adrenaline hits me and I reach for it, sliding my fingers around the cold metal. I know how to use one—my father insisted I learn because even though it wasn't expected that a woman would have one, she should at least know how to defend herself. About the only thing he and I agreed on.

'Tsk, tsk, *gattina,*' a dark male voice says from the doorway. 'Don't you know it's rude to go snooping about in other people's bedrooms?'

CHAPTER SIX

Vincenzo

CATERINA IS STANDING next to my bed with a gun in her hand, and I can see immediately from the way she's holding it, with the safety off, that she knows how to use it. Good. A wife who can't defend herself is a sitting duck. What is less good is that the instant I spoke, she lifted her hand and now the muzzle of the gun is pointing directly at me.

I fold my arms and lean against the door-frame, unbothered. She's not going to shoot me, I'm sure of it. She has a fiery temper but I know a killer when I see one and a killer she is not.

No, she's your wife, remember?

Oh, I've not forgotten. I might have spent the last hour or so organising for Annika to attend me tonight, as well as fielding more calls from my head of security to keep me updated on the Salvatores' response, but I'm well aware that I now have a wife.

Giovanni Salvatore has not given any answer to my ultimatum yet, but considering his daughter's life will be forfeit, I'm sure he will. I didn't give him much time, but that was intentional. I don't want him to think, I only want him to act on his paternal instincts.

Naturally, I'm not going kill Caterina—murdering one's wife only hours after marrying her is generally frowned upon, even among the families, not to mention rendering my little crusade utterly pointless—but Salvatore doesn't know that. All he knows is that one of the *cosa nostra's* most powerful bosses has his daughter and will kill her if he doesn't pledge his allegiance to me.

'Put the gun down, *gattina,*' I say. 'You're not going to shoot me.'

Her chin lifts, the gun still resolutely pointed at me. 'You don't know that.'

'Sadly, I do. I'm a killer, but you are not.'

She's out of her wedding finery now, wearing some loose black trousers and a green sweatshirt. Her glossy black hair has been put into a ponytail, long tendrils like black smoke clustering around her ears.

In the loose, shapeless clothes, she looks small and fragile, yet also beautiful, which I find odd. There's no hint of her figure and yet the green of the sweatshirt enhances the colour of her eyes, and the neck is wide enough to have fallen off one shoulder, revealing the line of a black bra strap and some smooth light-olive skin beneath it.

'No, I'm not,' she agrees. 'But it's never too late to start being one, right?'

'You could pull that trigger, it's true,' I say. 'But you wouldn't live long enough to enjoy your widowhood, alas. My security is…how shall I put it? Enthusiastic.'

Her hand is shaking a little, the muzzle wobbling, but she doesn't lower the gun. 'So what then? I'm just your prisoner forever? Is that what you're going to do with me?'

'Correction. You're my wife forever.'

She snorts. 'Is there a difference?'

I decide to ignore this, since I've yet to make specific plans about what to do with her. 'What are you doing in here, *gattina?*' I ask instead.

'What does it look like?' she snaps. 'I'm trying to get away from you.'

'By exploring my bedroom?'

She flushes even as green sparks of anger glitter in her eyes. Interesting. Is she blushing because I said the words 'my bedroom'? How delightful, if so. It's been a while since I've encountered such innocence in a woman.

'I thought I might find something useful,' she says. 'And as it turns out, I did.'

The gun, supposedly, which won't help her, as I've already pointed out. Even if she manages to get a shot at me, she'll then have to contend with all the guards in the villa, and there are a lot of them.

'Well,' I say calmly, 'as refreshing as it is to be held at gunpoint by my own wife, you're going to have to let me go at some stage.' I pause and then decide to mention it, since she'll find out anyway. 'At least before Annika arrives.'

Her eyes narrow. 'Annika? Who is Annika?'

I shift against the door-frame, oddly discomforted, though why I'm not sure. Caterina and I are married, it's true, but those vows of fidelity we swore were only words with no meaning behind them. I don't love her and she doesn't love me, and I'm going to make sure it stays that way, since love is a cruelty I wouldn't wish on my worst enemy. At some stage, though, I might want to explore that moment of chemistry we had during our wedding ceremony, but not now.

I ignore my discomfort. 'She's my mistress,' I say bluntly. 'I'm expecting a wedding night, after all.'

'Mistress?' She says the word as if it's foreign to her and she's unsure of the pronunciation. 'What are you? Seventy? Who has mistresses these days?'

I can't help but smile at the disbelief in her voice. '*I* have mistresses. Don't you think the term is more romantic than, say, "lover"?'

'Romantic?' Again, she says it as if she's never heard the word before. 'Are you serious? You've just married me and you're already talking about lovers?'

I study her a moment, because the shock on her face looks genuine. How strange. Why should she care how many lovers I take? Shouldn't she be pleased that I'm not going to take advantage of her? That I'm seeking pleasure elsewhere?

'What does that matter?' I ask. 'I already told you I'm not expecting you in my bed. All I want from you is your name and your father's obedience.'

Expressions move over her face like clouds, moving so fast I can't read them all. 'So…what do you expect from me? I mean, are you going to get an annulment in six months or what?'

I haven't told her my plans. I'm waiting for her father's capitulation first, but it won't hurt to tell her now. Perhaps it will make her lower that fucking gun.

'I expect you to be my wife,' I say simply. 'As I said, it has to be you to ensure your father's obedience. But I also need a wife to start a family with, building my dynasty, etc., etc.'

'That might be difficult if we're not sharing a bed.' She goes pink as she says this, which again, I find strangely delightful.

'I presume you've heard of the existence of fertility clinics?' I murmur, then add, unable to help myself, 'Or of course there is the old-fashioned way.'

Her cheeks flush an even deeper rose, but her mouth firms. 'No. My statement about the goat still stands.'

'Pity.' I sigh theatrically, enjoying myself more than I care to admit. 'I could wear a goat costume at a pinch.'

I'm hoping to get a smile out of her since she's managed to get so many out of me, but her mouth remains in a firm line. 'So, I'm what? Just a figurehead? What about me? What about what I want?'

Unfortunately, the answer is that I didn't care what she wanted. But again she's forcing me to contend with the fact that she's a person. It's inconvenient. I don't want her thoughts and feelings getting in the way of my crusade, because nothing can get in the way of my crusade.

I will stop the murders of blameless women and children, stop the inter-family killings. I will stop the men who think violence is the answer, men like my father, and I will not be turned from my path. I will not be stopped, not by anyone, and she needs to understand that.

'What about you?' I ask, allowing a chill to enter my voice. 'What you want doesn't concern me.'

Her gaze narrows even further, turning calculating, which is fascinating, though I'm not sure why. Perhaps it's because while I can read most of her emotions, I can't tell what she's actually thinking, and it's strange to realise that I want to know. 'So, if I wanted to take a lover myself you wouldn't care?' she asks, the gun still firmly pointed at me.

A sharp feeling knifes through me and it takes me a second to process what it is. Jealousy. But no, surely not? I'm territorial, it's true, but as long as she's discreet, what does it matter if she takes a lover? I don't care. My father was a jealous man, but I am not.

Yet a part of me, the wolf, cares and it's insisting that she's mine. It won't tolerate another male anywhere near her.

Her sharp green eyes glitter and I know she's spotted my hesitation, and before I can speak, she says, 'As per usual, a man is free to do whatever he wants, but not a woman.' The muzzle of the gun lowers slowly from my face, tracking a line right down to...*fuck*. 'How would you feel if I shot off your dick?' She's all determination now. 'Not so manly now, hmmm?'

The wolf in me growls in approval at her bravado, but the man is not amused. In fact, the man is now actively pissed off, because this ridiculous conversation has been going on much longer than he wanted, and he has things to do.

'You can have lovers,' I say impatiently, crushing my strange jealous feelings. 'You can have as many as you want, I don't give a fuck.'

'Yes, you do,' she disagrees. 'Don't deny it, I saw you hesitate.'

'Caterina,' I begin.

'I don't trust you,' she says, ignoring me. 'So, know this. If you don't want me to have lovers, then you can't have any either.'

I give a short laugh and take a step into the room, my patience rapidly thinning. 'I'm not a monk, *gattina,* and I have no intention of living like one.'

She doesn't move, the gun still pointed in the direction of my fly. 'Well, you'll have to figure out how, won't you?'

My anger flares and holding her gaze with mine, I take another step. 'Are you sure that's a good idea?' I ask silkily. 'That would mean living under the same roof as a very hungry wolf. Who sees you as prey.'

Her eyes widen as she understands my meaning. The colour of them is truly astonishing, green as grass and with gold glittering in the heart of them.

I take another step, halfway to her by now, and she doesn't seem to realise that I'm stalking her. Coming slowly closer to grab the gun from her hand. At least, that was my plan, but now I'm fascinated by the colour of her eyes. So green, they can't be real. Pretty, pretty eyes.

The gun shakes slightly, but she doesn't look away. Her pupils are dilating and now I can see the pulse at the base of her throat, just above the neckline of her sweatshirt. It's racing. Is it with fear? Or something else?

She swallows. 'Y-you said you didn't want me in your bed.'

'Perhaps I do.' I take another step. 'In the absence of anyone else, I could be persuaded.'

'Stop,' she says, her voice husky.

But I don't stop, because I'm already there, reaching out to take the gun from her shaking hands as she stares up at me, eyes wide, pupils fully darkened with something that definitely isn't fear.

Except she doesn't let go of the gun. Despite those wide eyes, nothing is going to deter her. 'Cancel your mistress,' she says. 'Do it.'

I could pull the gun from her hands, it wouldn't be difficult. But the safety is off and I'm not fully convinced she wouldn't actually shoot me by accident, so I don't take it. Instead I ask, 'Why?' And it's a genuine question, because I don't understand why this particular thing is important to her.

'You married me,' she says. 'You didn't have to, but you did, so you have to bear the consequences. And those are that you respect me enough not to screw another woman on our wedding night.'

CHAPTER SEVEN

Caterina

HE'S HOLDING ONTO the gun with strong fingers and surely he must know he could pull it out of my grip at any time and with ease. But he's not.

He's a terrifying figure standing so close, towering over me in a way that most men don't since I'm tall for a woman. But it's not just his height, it's the width of his powerful shoulders and the breadth of his chest. He's hard-muscled and strong, and I don't know why any part of me is noticing that, but it is. Just as it's noticing that scent of smoke and cedar too, warm and musky and masculine.

He hypnotised me with his silver gaze, stalking me slowly, and even though I wanted to, I couldn't make my finger pull the trigger.

I don't know what I'm trying to get out of him, because why should I care if he wants to sleep with his mistress tonight? Maybe it's only that with the gun, I can get some power back, because he has it all. I want him to acknowledge me as a person, not just a pawn he's using in his game with my father, because I'm so tired of being that pawn.

I want him to understand what he's doing to me in marrying me. I want him to know that I have opinions and thoughts and dreams, and he's just another man taking them all away from me.

And okay, maybe it's true. Maybe I really don't want him to sleep with his mistress on our wedding night, even though it shouldn't matter.

Still, one thing I do know is that with this gun in my hand, I'm powerful. I can make him do what I want for a change, even if that power is only an illusion since he's right. I'm not a killer. I'm not like him, not in any way.

I only wanted to prove myself and now that I have, I finally lower the gun, click on the safety, and extend it to him.

He blinks in surprise, before looking down at the weapon as if he doesn't know what it is.

'Go on,' I say. 'You wanted it. Take it.'

He doesn't though. Instead he looks at me. 'Why? I thought you wanted to shoot me, *gattina.*'

'I changed my mind.' Oddly, I feel more powerful now the gun has been lowered than when I was holding it. Perhaps that's because I finally did something that surprised him again, made him take notice, and that feels...good. 'Go on.' I shake the weapon at him. 'Take it.'

He takes it from my hand, checks it over with a practiced, reflexive movement. 'What about your deal?' he asks. 'I was about to capitulate, but then you went and gave away your advantage.'

'You were right.' I clasp my hands together so he can't see how they shake. 'I don't care what you do with another woman.'

He glances down at the gun again, a thoughtful expression on his handsome face. 'No, I don't think I was right,' he says slowly. 'I think you were.' His gaze lifts to mine. 'What you said about respect is true. You're my wife and as such, you are worthy of mine. Which means it would be disrespectful to sleep with Annika tonight.'

A small shock goes through me. I'm not expecting him to capitulate, not at all, so all I do is stare at him and ask stupidly, 'What?'

'I'm going to cancel Annika.' He's decisive as he puts the gun down on the bed then gets out his phone. 'Tonight you and I will have dinner instead.'

I open my mouth to tell him I don't want to have dinner with him, but he's already turning away. 'Six thirty,' he says over his shoulder. 'Maria will come and get you.' Then he strides out of the bedroom, the sound of his deep voice echoing in the hallway as he talks to whomever he just called. Annika, presumably.

I'm still trembling, my heart banging against my ribs, and I don't know if I'm afraid or thrilled. Afraid that he changed his mind about Annika and wants dinner with me instead, or thrilled that I managed to change his mind about her and wants dinner with me instead.

Go on, you're thrilled.

I take a deep breath, staring blankly at the gun on the bed. Maybe I *am* thrilled. He's ruthless and single-minded in his goals, and I've had first-hand experience of exactly how single-minded he is. And yet… I got him to change his mind, and I don't think it was just because I'd threatened his manhood. No, he changed it because of what I said about respect.

The families are obsessed with respect and who is owed it and whether they deserve it, etc., etc. And Vincenzo Argenti is obviously no exception. Then again, he didn't say I was worthy of respect, he said I was worthy of *his* respect.

Which is interesting. Certainly within the families, no one can disrespect another man's wife. But a husband can disrespect his own wife, that's perfectly allowable, and I've seen it happen many times. I was too young to remember what my father's relationship with my mother was like before she died, but whenever he spoke about her, it wasn't with grief that she was dead, it was more about the insult to his and our family's honour.

I can't imagine Vincenzo Argenti actually respecting anyone, let alone the woman he kidnapped and forced into marriage, but when his gaze met mine, I had the feeling he was being genuine.

I don't want to keep thinking about him, though. I don't want him taking up so much space in my head, so I push the thoughts away. Instead I pause over the gun, wondering whether I should take it with me, but in the end I leave it on the bed. He wasn't wrong when he said if I shoot him, I wouldn't last long enough to enjoy my widowhood. His security is insane and I'm certainly not in the mood to die purely for the satisfaction of putting a bullet between his eyes.

Dinner is still a couple of hours away, so I spend time exploring the rest of the villa. It's stunningly beautiful, the gardens, the lawns, the terraces with pots overflowing with herbs and flowers. But through all this beauty it's impossible to see anything but a cage. There are too many men dressed in black and wearing sunglasses, just randomly walking around. Patrolling the grounds. It makes sense. This plan to unite the families under his rule will have made him many enemies.

I ponder this as I go inside and find a gorgeous little library on the ground floor. It looks over yet another terrace and into some rose gardens, with shelves that are floor to high, vaulted ceiling and a fireplace to warm the room. I wander idly over to the shelves and inspect the spines, thinking about the plan he mentioned in the car in Rome, of bringing the warring factions under one command like he's a medieval king. I would have said that's impossible, but I do know from what my father has said, that he's already brought half the families under his control.

Stop the killings, the Wolf told me. *That's what I want to do.*

It's admirable, I have to admit as I take out another book and examine the cover. But what makes him think the killings would stop under *his* rule? Does he think he's better or more moral than everyone else?

What do you care?

I shove the book back onto the shelf with a little more force than strictly necessary, annoyed by the thought. I *don't* care. I really don't. I want to get *out* of the world I was brought up in. I want to be a normal twenty-five-year-old, with a job and a boyfriend, and live in a flat with a cat.

I don't want to go from one prison to another, to become yet another man's property. I'm tired of it. And I'm tired of feeling powerless, too.

You had some power up in his bedroom.

I turn away from the bookcases, still thinking. It was true, I did. I got him to change his mind, though that might have been the gun. Then again, he changed his mind *after* I gave him the weapon, so maybe it wasn't the gun after all. Maybe it was me. If so, perhaps I can get him to change his mind about other things too, such as letting me go.

I make my way slowly upstairs to my room, because dinner will be soon, and I need to decide what kind of woman I want to be when I meet him again. Do I want to be Cat in sweatpants and sweatshirt? Or Cat in full wifely make-up and dress?

I go over to the closet and slide open the doors, examining the clothes on the rack. Part of me wants to stay in what I'm wearing and he can go to hell with his expensive dresses and stupid lacy underwear. But another part of me is whispering that he might be expecting me *not* to make an effort, so why not surprise him? Or maybe he's expecting full make-up and ball gown, so a sweatshirt is the better surprise?

I stand there looking at the gowns and dresses, paralysed by my own indecision, which is ridiculous, because it's only a dinner.

Remind him again that you're his wife. That you deserve respect.

I blink at the thought. It's true. If I'm demanding his respect I need to look like the wife he's expecting me to be. I need to remind him of the consequences of what he's done by bringing me here and marrying me immediately. If he thought he could put a ring on my finger, legally marry me, then forget about me and lock me away like a trophy in his cabinet, then he'll soon find out he's wrong.

Determination fills me and I reach for a cocktail dress without hesitation. It's emerald green and has so many sequins it's like a disco ball, but when I put it on and look at myself in the mirror, I don't actually look like a disco ball.

The green fabric shimmers and sparkles as it clings to my body, outlining every curve. The neckline is plunging and there is a slit in one side that cuts straight up my thigh to my hip. It's sexy as hell and as much as I hate to admit it, it fits me perfectly.

I take my hair out of its ponytail and shake it out, letting the long straight length of it fall over my shoulders. The treatments the hairdresser put in it in preparation for the wedding have made it look glossy and silky. I've never really bothered with it before, but now I'm bothering and I'm pleased.

Still, if I'm going to go full wife, I need make-up, and since I hate wearing make-up, it's going to be a challenge to get it looking perfect. But half an hour and a few YouTube tutorials later, I've managed to get mascara on my lashes with no clumps, and gold and green eye shadow on my lids without fallout. Then it's a slick of red lip balm on my lips for that freshly bitten look, and some high-heeled golden sandals that make my legs look like they go on forever.

By the time I'm done, it's nearly six thirty, and nerves are gathering in my gut. But I'm not going to wait for Maria to come for me, oh no, I'll be damned if I wait on his order. So, I give myself one last going-over, then I turn from the mirror and head out of the room.

CHAPTER EIGHT

Vincenzo

I'VE ORGANISED FOR Maria to serve us dinner out on the terrace that overlooks the sea, and she's done a fine job. The table is set with a white tablecloth, the finest crystal champagne flutes, heavy silver cutlery and a bottle of Dom Perignon in an ice bucket. Candles in elegant glass holders flicker in the slight sea-breeze, and the bougainvillea that cascades from the terrace above in a riot of pink, hangs picturesquely over the scene.

And as I stand there surveying the scene, a part of me is wondering why the hell I'm fussing around with place settings and candles for my new forced bride, when I could be in bed screwing Annika.

It's a complete fucking mystery.

Everything about my behaviour since I kidnapped Caterina Salvatore seems to be a complete fucking mystery, and I hate mysteries.

I always know what I'm doing and everything is in service to my goal of cleaning the tarnish from the Argenti family's honour. Deciding to cancel my evening with Annika in favour of dinner with my new wife is not cleaning any tarnish from the Argenti family's honour. It's got nothing to do with anyone's honour at all, so I don't know why I did it.

She said I had to bear the consequences of marrying her, that I owe her the respect of at least not screwing another woman on our wedding night, and I…had to admit to myself that she was right.

It was a simple thing she'd asked of me. Nothing to do with giving her freedom or sparing her father's life, only a little respect for one night. Then, of course, without waiting for a response, she gave up her only weapon to me. As if she'd made her point and didn't need it anymore.

Ridiculous creature. In that moment, with her untidy ponytail and her sweatshirt half falling off her shoulder and her loose black trousers, she looked young, vulnerable and fragile. Defenceless. The perfect prey for the predator. And I was the predator. I was the villain. Yet she gave up her weapon without even waiting for an answer, and that made something in me catch and pull, like a fish hook catching on a rock.

A wife in the families is a host, a mediator, she runs the household and takes care of the children. She is guarded and protected, staying out of the business side of things, because that is a job for men.

My mother, Elena, was different, at least at the start. She was fiery, opinionated, fiercely protective and loyal. Yet, over the years, my father slowly ground all those things out of her. He would not tolerate any exceptions to the norm and he would not tolerate those who wouldn't do what he said. His word was law. My mother didn't fit into the box he put her in, so he made her fit by cutting away the pieces of her he didn't like.

I assumed that any wife I eventually had would be exactly like all the rest. A good *cosa nostra* wife who supports her husband, but I knew upstairs in that bedroom, that Caterina Salvatore would not be a wife like all the rest.

She's like my mother, full of fire and spark, and the way she challenged me with the gun and with her wit...

My father didn't respect my mother, not at all. He had mistresses scattered from one end of Italy to the other, and he visited them all while she remained here at the estate, dependent on the drugs the doctors fed her.

I'm supposed to be different. I'm supposed to be better. A more honourable man than he ever was, and so how could I do anything but give her what she wanted?

I suspect there's more to it than that, especially because I didn't feel even the slightest bit of disappointment about cancelling Annika. But I don't want to think about what more there is. Not now. Not when I'm still waiting for Giovanni Salvatore's sworn loyalty.

I can even admit to some...anticipation at the thought of having dinner with my strangely fascinating new wife. She certainly won't be boring, at least.

Turning from my survey of the table, I'm about to find Maria to tell her to summon my wife, when a woman walks through the French doors and out onto the terrace as if she owns it.

She's tall and built like a dancer, long legs, slim hips, small, rounded breasts, each and every curve followed lovingly by the fabric of her green sequinned dress. Her black hair is loose down her back, falling almost to her waist, and her incredible eyes are highlighted with sparkles of gold and green on her lids. She wears high-heeled golden sandals that make her legs even longer, and the basest part of me imagines having those long legs wrapped around my waist as I fuck her. Or maybe flung over my shoulders, the long spike of her heel digging into my back as I make her come.

The woman is unfamiliar at first and I have the passing thought that maybe she's one of my other lovers and if so, what is she doing here? Then, like a blurred scene through a camera lens suddenly springing into focus, I realise who the woman is.

She's my wife. Caterina.

She is cool and self-contained as she stands a moment, studying the terrace, the table, and then me. And when her gaze meets mine I feel the impact, all glittering, sharp-edged challenge.

The wolf in me shifts, hungry, predatory, knowing exactly what it wants to eat now and it's not the food Maria will be serving us. Before in sweatshirt and pants, she looked vulnerable and fragile, and the wolf wanted to protect her.

But right here, right now, in her green sequins and war paint, the wolf wants to fuck her. And so do I.

'I'm early, sorry,' she says, not sounding sorry in the least. 'I didn't want to wait for Maria.'

I move instantly, rounding the table to pull out her chair for her. 'Nor should you. Please. Sit.'

She stalks over to the chair, eyeing me warily, perhaps expecting me to stand back to let her sit down. But I don't. There's a reason she's all dressed up with looks to kill, and there's a reason her make-up is war paint.

She's on a mission, this little *gattina*, that's obvious, and I'm fascinated to discover what kind of mission she's on. Is it to prove she can be the perfect wife like all the others? Or is it to show me exactly what kind of woman I married? Or is it that she knows I want her and is going to use that to get what she wants out of me?

Intriguing woman. The dress and the make-up are pure *cosa nostra* wife, but that look of stubborn determination in her eyes... I've seen that same look in the eyes of my paternal grandmother before she died. All steel, no mercy. The woman who made my father what he was. The look of a warrior.

I hold the sides of her chair as she sits down, and I catch her scent, warm jasmine and musk, and the wolf in me growls, hungry and getting hungrier. I glance down at the top of her glossy black head, noticing that despite her confident entry, her shoulders are tense and there's a stiffness to her movements.

So, this is all an act to hide her nerves. Yet, seeing through her bravado doesn't disappoint me. It only makes me respect her even more. She came to this mission ready, despite being afraid, and she came down to face me. And I am not an easy man to face.

I let go of her chair and walk over to the ice bucket where the bottle of Dom is sitting atop a mound of ice. 'A little of this excellent champagne to celebrate,' I say, opening the foil then popping the cork.

'To celebrate what?' Her voice is sharp. 'My kidnapping?'

'Of course.' I ignore her tone, pouring us out two glasses and then handing one to her. 'And our marriage.'

She takes it, watching me as I sit opposite her. 'To my new wife.' I lift my glass in a toast.

Her eyes glitter in the candlelight, green as the sequins on her dress. 'You'll forgive me if I don't drink to my own imprisonment.'

'A little dramatic, *gattina,*' I chide, mostly for my own amusement. 'You're hardly a prisoner.'

'Aren't I?' She puts her glass down, untouched. 'There are guards on basically every square meter of this entire property.'

'Of course there are guards.' I take a sip of the champagne and it is, indeed, excellent. 'I'm the head of the Argenti family and I have enemies. They're there to keep people out, not in.'

'So, if I wanted to, say, take a helicopter tomorrow and get out of here, I could?'

Oh, she's sharp as the points of her little heels isn't she?

My pulse accelerates as I smile and settle back into my chair, enjoying the challenge she's just thrown at me, and anticipating more. 'Naturally you could. Providing you have adequate security.'

Her gaze narrows. 'And if I didn't want security?'

'Come now, *gattina*. You know how this works. I'm sure your father didn't let you go anywhere without a bodyguard or three, so why would you expect that to change now you're my wife? You're still a target, I'm afraid.'

It's no less than the truth, but it's clear she doesn't like that one bit.

'I've been a prisoner in my father's house all my life,' she says flatly. 'And I refuse to be one here. So if what you said about respecting me is true, then you need to respect my need to feel like I live here, not like I'm trapped here.'

She's so very emphatic, her gaze never wavering from mine, the force of her will measuring itself against my own. It makes my pulse beat even faster. I like it. I like her challenge and her spirit. I like her courage and her ferocity. She's gutsy, this woman, to come downstairs dressed like that, ready to cross swords with me, knowing who and what I am.

But she's right. She is *trapped here. Just like your mother was.*

Something tightens in my chest, but I ignore the feeling. This is an entirely different situation. Caterina is *not* trapped here. She can leave at any time, as long as she has some security.

Besides, I can't imagine her being anyone's prisoner. How her father even got her to the altar to marry the Bianchi stripling seems like a miracle. Unless she wanted to be there, of course.

It's another question to ask her, but I'm getting distracted. Because the electricity we both felt during that moment of our wedding ceremony is filling the air again. It's making her eyes widen and pupils dilate, her red lips parting.

The wolf in me wants to get rid of the table between us, snatch her up from her chair and rip her dress clean off, put her down on the ground and make her mine completely. But I'm not a teenage boy with no control over himself, and the wolf doesn't control me either, so I fight it.

The wolf is merely an aspect of myself that came into being after I was punished for my failure to kill the entire Salvatore family. In the dank little room in the basement of this villa, my father gave me scars to ensure I never forgot what it was to disappoint him. And in that very same room I became the predator I needed to be in order to take him down eventually. A wolf to protect those who were mine and to hunt down those who were not.

Yet the wolf is not in charge. I am. And I'm not giving into it yet. My new wife clearly has no love for me, though her body might disagree, and I'm not in the mood to change her mind tonight. If I want sex that badly, I can wait and see Annika tomorrow, or maybe the night after. It doesn't have to be now.

'You're very demanding for a kidnapped woman,' I murmur. 'Especially when I'm still waiting for your father to give me his loyalty on pain of your death.'

She says nothing, sitting stiff in her chair, that gaze of hers not letting up.

I take a sip of my champagne and then glance over

the terrace at the view of the sun sinking majestically into the sea. 'Sundown is approaching very rapidly.'

Her jaw is tight, every line of her body tense. 'And if he doesn't give it? You'll kill me?'

Surely she can't still think that I would? When I saved her all those years ago? When I told her in the car back in Rome that if I wanted her dead, she would be?

'Of course not, *gattina*,' I say with some impatience. 'I've already made that very clear. But your father doesn't know that.'

Her thick black lashes flutter and abruptly she looks down at the white tablecloth, lovely mouth in a grim line. 'He hasn't given it yet?'

'No,' I confirm, studying her.

She nods and swallows, keeping her gaze on the table. The flickering of the candlelight betrays her, though. I can see the sheen of tears in her eyes, and it hits me somewhere I wasn't expecting. Somewhere… painful.

A woman's tears have never moved me before, so why they're doing so now, I have no idea. Perhaps it's because I don't like to see a woman with so much spirit and fire in pain. Again, it reminds me of my mother, slowly fading before my eyes as my father kept her trapped here in the villa, using her as his brood mare when it suited him, ignoring her when it didn't.

'You're upset,' I say, not liking her distress.

She doesn't look at me, only blinks furiously. 'No, I'm not.'

I ignore her. 'Are you afraid for him? Or are you afraid for yourself?'

She continues to look at the tablecloth for a long moment. Then, quite abruptly, she looks up at me and I can see pain in her eyes. But also something else.

Fury again. It smoulders in her eyes like a hot, green coal.

'He won't give you his loyalty,' she says. 'He'd rather let me die. I'm a pawn to him, nothing more.'

Her anger colours every word, matching the heat in her eyes, and she throws them at me like spears, each sharp point finding their mark.

I know exactly what it means to be only a pawn to one's father. That's all I was too. After my mother retreated to her bedroom for good, he took charge of me, though *I* didn't matter to him as much as the fact that I was his heir. I had to look like him and talk like him, make the decisions he would make. If I stepped out of line even slightly, I was punished for it.

But isn't that how you've been treating her too? Like a pawn?

A cold current of awareness winds through me. Yes, it's true and I've acknowledged it more than once. But putting my thoughts about her in the context of my own father's behaviour is...disturbing.

Again, I'm *not* him and I never was. Once, perhaps, after my mother died and he was the only family I had left, I wanted to be the perfect son for him. But then he ordered me to kill a child and everything changed. As I took the punishment he doled out, his spiked belt gouging holes in my flesh as he laid it across my back, that's when I decided he was a stain on the honour of the Argentis. A stain that needed to be cleaned, and that I would be the one to clean it. I would be the one to set a new example of what the head of a family could be, a better example.

How is the way you're treating her better?

She sits across the table from me, that fury in her eyes glowing hot, and along with it the pain, and I understand all at once that the way I'm treating her is *not* better. That to actually be a better man and not merely paying lip service to the idea, I need to change my thinking. I need to change how I treat her.

I don't look away. 'What makes you think you're only a pawn?'

'Because he told me so. Basically every day since my mother and brother died. He blamed me for their deaths.'

I frown, puzzled by this. 'How could he do that? You were only a child.'

Caterina's gaze is level. 'Yes. But I was also the only one who survived.'

CHAPTER NINE

Caterina

He's lounging in the chair opposite, his long, muscled body relaxed. Like a panther. He's in black suit trousers and a black shirt with the first couple of buttons undone. He wears no jewellery except the heavy gold signet ring that he took off to give to me so I had a ring to put on his finger.

He's almost monklike in the severity of his clothes, yet no monk looks like he does. The candlelight loves his high carved cheek bones, the straight length of his nose, and that mouth of his that seemed so cruel before, isn't now. No, now it's beautiful. *He*'s beautiful, with his silver-grey eyes and his intense stare.

My heart is beating so damn fast and it won't slow down. I hadn't meant to tell him about my relationship with my father or to fling that confession like a vase at his head. I didn't want him to know how upset I was, but when he reminded me that his deadline for my father's loyalty is sundown tonight, I couldn't seem to find my nice, polite, well-bred Salvatore mask.

Because that sun is going down and if my father

hasn't given the Wolf his loyalty by now, he's not going to give it. Which is only confirmation—as if my whole damn life wasn't confirmation enough—that my father doesn't care about me. Not one single iota.

I should have expected it, but expectations and reality seldom meet, and so my own reaction caught me by surprise. The tears mainly, because I didn't want to feel sad about it. I wanted to be angry, since anger is so much more powerful. Dad never had any patience with my anger, said it wasn't becoming in a woman, yet anger is what I cling to, because he can go to hell.

Vincenzo Argenti can go to hell too, though I have to admit, he doesn't seem to have an issue with my fury. No, he's staring back at me as if I've fascinated him in some way.

You like it.

A part of me does. A part of me finds that very powerful.

'He wasn't pleased you survived?' the Wolf asks, his voice cool and detached sounding.

It's wrong to talk to him about my family and our relationships with each other, since technically he's the enemy. But over the years my family loyalty has been steadily worn away by my father's contempt, and besides, this man is my husband now. I'm going to give him my family history whether he wants it or not.

'No,' I say bluntly. 'He wanted my mother and brother to be the ones who lived. My brother, because Alessio was his heir, and my mother because she could make more heirs. I was an afterthought child. A daughter as a sop to my mother.'

'Sounds familiar,' the Wolf murmurs, though he doesn't elaborate on what exactly sounds familiar. 'He didn't think to make you his heir?'

'Of course not. I'm a woman. My only use was in making alliances.'

Out beyond the terrace, on the horizon, the sun flares as it readies itself to disappear into the sea. My father won't pledge his loyalty to the Wolf. His dream of vengeance against the Argenti threat is more important to him than the life of his one remaining child, and despite myself and my fury, the little girl I used to be feels as if a knife has been plunged into her chest. My mother loved me and so did my brother, and when they died, I lost the only two people who thought I was important. The only people to whom I mattered. And it makes me feel the ache of their loss all over again.

It's his fault. His family's fault.

It would be easy to blame him and the Argentis. That's what my father did. But my father was also the one who ordered the killing of this man's mother for some petty slight lost in the mists of time, so can the fault really lie with the Argentis?

I don't know anymore, but perhaps there's something to the Wolf's aim of stopping the inter-family killings.

He's studying me intently, something in his eyes I can't name. Has my story affected him? It's intrigued him, that's for sure.

'Well,' he murmurs at last, a dark and heated note in his voice that makes me want to shiver. 'Your father's a fool then.'

Surprise ripples through me. 'Why do you say that?'

'Because he missed an opportunity. You have a lot of courage, *gattina*, not to mention determination and spirit, and those are valuable qualities to have in the head of a family, regardless of gender.'

Praise from the Wolf shouldn't make a wave of warmth roll through me, yet it does. I haven't been called anything but disobedient, wilful and a damn nuisance for years, and so a part of me laps up his words like a flower starved of sunlight.

There's a lump in my throat and I don't want him to see how he's touched me, so I reach for my glass and take a healthy sip of champagne instead. The liquid is yeasty and cold, and delicious, so I take another, even though I shouldn't drink it too fast. Getting tipsy here in this literal wolf's den would not be a good idea.

'My father would disagree.' I make myself put down the champagne glass. 'Clearly he's not going to give you his loyalty tonight. Which puts you in the difficult position of having to kill your new wife.' I lift my gaze to his and hold it. 'Good thing we didn't have a proper wedding.'

His handsome features are enigmatic, his gaze glittering. I can't tell what he's thinking. He's been saying he wouldn't kill me all this time, and so far, he hasn't. Perhaps he won't. Still, I can't take his word for anything, can I? He's not only the enemy, he's been my personal nightmare ever since I was a child, and regardless that his bullets didn't kill my mother and brother, he was still sent to our family's door to kill us. Also, he did say to me up in his bedroom that he was a killer.

Fear is a cold snake in my gut, but I don't let it out. I pile anger on instead. Anger is strong and powerful. *Let him try and do it,* I think. *I'll go down fighting him every step of the way.*

'*Gattina,*' he murmurs eventually, putting down his wine glass. 'How many times must I tell you? I am not going to hurt you. I didn't save you only to kill you twenty years later. What would be the point in that?'

'Why should I believe you?' I try to make it sound like a question yet it comes out sounding like a demand instead. 'Your father wanted my entire family dead.'

'That is true,' he concedes. 'But I am not my father. And it's this inter-family violence that I'm trying to stop.' He pauses a moment, his gaze on me intensifying. 'I'm not going to hurt you, Caterina. I give you my word.'

I shouldn't believe him. I shouldn't trust him as far as I could throw him, not when he hasn't given me any reason to. Yet… I see the truth in his eyes now. He means it. He means every word. This is a solemn vow, as binding as an oath.

The tightly coiled snake in my gut relaxes a little, and I let out a breath. 'But you told my father you would. Not following through on a threat isn't going to make you look good.'

'Oh, I'm going to follow through on it.' The corner of his mouth curves. 'At least as far as your father is concerned.'

'What do you mean?'

'You wouldn't be the first woman I've "killed" who then turns up later with a new identity.'

At first I don't understand and then his meaning penetrates. 'You mean you'll…what? Fake my death?'

He lifts one powerful shoulder. 'Yes. And I can usually produce some very convincing evidence, too.'

'So you've done it before?'

He gives a quiet laugh that feels as if it's rolling over my skin like soft, dark velvet. 'Many times. I want to stop the violence, the killing of innocents, but sometimes the so-called deaths of innocents must be staged in order to ensure compliance. Some of those innocents did not appreciate their new lives, but since it's better than actual death, they somehow survived.'

The Wolf of Sicily has had many deaths laid at his door in his ruthless grab for power, that's well-known. Women, children. He's supposed to have no boundaries, which makes this confession so surprising I don't know what to say.

He smiles, a warm and genuine one this time. 'Look at that,' he murmurs. 'I've finally shocked you.'

'But…' I manage. 'Why?'

'I might be many things, *gattina,* but one thing I'm not is a hypocrite.' That beautiful smile slowly fades, the intensity in his eyes burning bright. 'The killing will end if it's the last thing I do.'

The force of his conviction and the almost palpable nature of his will should be frightening, yet I'm not frightened. I'm fascinated by why the head of the most powerful *cosa nostra* family in Europe has suddenly come to value human lives when he never has before, at least not on the face of it.

'Why?' I'm probably too blunt, but who cares? I want to know. 'I mean, that's not what everyone says about you. You're famous for having—'

'No morals or boundaries?' he finishes for me. 'A carefully cultivated lie, once again propagated to ensure compliance.' He shifts in his chair, a wolf settling into his den, studying me from across the white tablecloth. 'Though, once it was true. At least it was until I saw you with your terrified eyes.' Impossibly, his gaze gets even more intense, holding me captive as surely as iron chains. 'Because of you, Caterina, I found my line in the sand. And because of your mother and brother's deaths, I decided that I could not let the pointless killing of people go on. It has to end somewhere and I decided it would end with me.'

I thought I could not possibly get any more shocked, but apparently, I'm wrong. He can't mean that, can he? It seemed ridiculous in the car back in Rome and it seems just as ridiculous here on the terrace now. That me, a five-year-old girl, could change the entire course of a man's life just by looking up at him in fear?

'B-but…' I break off, not able to think of a word to say.

Again, that fascinating mouth of his curves in amusement. He does seem to like shocking me. 'It's true,' he says simply, correctly reading my disbelief. 'My father was very unhappy with me.'

I blink. Oh, of course. There would have been repercussions for him, wouldn't there? Stefano Argenti was not a merciful man, by all accounts.

'What did he do to you?' I ask point-blank.

The Wolf's smile changes, bitterness entering into it now. 'He punished me quite severely for my failure to kill you and your father. But don't worry, I got my own back.' His voice has deepened, roughened and again I can hear the darkness in it. 'My father died as he lived. By the sword.'

A cold shiver ripples over my skin. Even though he hasn't said anything explicitly, I know that somehow he had a hand in his father's death. And all at once, I'm aware that this is a very dangerous conversation to be having and with a very dangerous man. A man who has said he won't kill me, but no matter what he said about staging the deaths of innocents, he's certainly killed others.

The sun has now vanished below the horizon, lighting the sky on fire, and it's beautiful. And here I am on my wedding night, sitting and drinking champagne with my new husband, who perhaps won't kill me after all. Having just been given up by my father who indeed didn't care if I lived or died.

The pain in my heart aches as the light fades, the child in me hurting at the abandonment even as the adult woman is furious for having even a shred of hope that he might care. That the only people who ever loved me are dead and have been dead for years.

'Don't cry for him, *gattina,*' the Wolf says quietly and unexpectedly. 'He's not worth your tears. This isn't abandonment. This is the moment you're set free.'

There's a lump in my throat and I have to swallow more champagne to get rid of it, but he's not wrong. My father doesn't want me. I'm dead to him. Which means I finally have what I've always craved, which is to be free of him.

I look across the table at my husband. 'So, where does that leave you?'

'It leaves me with staging your death and perhaps organising you a new identity.' He shrugs. 'I'd hoped to avoid more bloodshed, but your father has chosen his path. He will come to regret it, I assure you.'

I should feel regret myself at this, but regret is hard to come by now my father has decided my life isn't worth as much as his pride. 'You'll have to find yourself another wife,' I say.

He tilts his head. 'Do I? A pity. You're starting to grow on me.'

Another wave of warmth rushes through me, and my cheeks heat. I'm not sure why I'm blushing. What do I care if I'm starting to grow on him or not? He kidnapped me and forced me to marry him, and regardless of that strange electricity between us, I shouldn't *like* that he likes me, right?

Except he's beautiful and powerful, and very dangerous, and something wild in me is pleased I've managed to affect him. The girl even her own father abandoned has somehow managed to make this powerful head of a *cosa nostra* family like her.

The air around us thickens, tension gathering, the force of his gaze like a hurricane wind, and my mind blanks. All I can see are his eyes and the silver flames in them, and all I can hear is my heart beating faster and faster.

I remember the light touch of his fingers as he straightened my tiara at our wedding ceremony, and the brush of his fingertip on my ear as he pushed a strand of hair behind it. The prickle of electricity that chased over my skin. The press of his mouth on my forehead, a feather-light kiss that I can still feel burning even now. And I'm looking at his mouth and the fullness of his bottom lip, and how it curves. Cruel and beautiful at the same time.

What would a real kiss from him be like?

The thought blazes in my head and now it's occurred to me, I can't stop thinking about it. That mouth not on my forehead, but on my lips. My first kiss. Would it feel as hot? What would he taste like? I remember the way he picked me up in the church earlier, throwing me over his shoulder like I weighed nothing. He was so hard, like stone, and yet warm, too.

Yet more heat steals through my cheeks, and I can't stop it, and suddenly this all feels too much. The danger in our conversation, my own honesty, the tears in my eyes that I know he saw, and him, sitting there, seeing my blush and knowing why. Because of course he'd know why.

I can't deal with it, not now, so I push myself to my feet, say 'excuse me' in a breathless voice, then I flee the terrace.

CHAPTER TEN

Vincenzo

I'M HALF OUT of my chair to stop her before I know what I'm doing. But when I realise, I force myself to sit back down. I've never chased a woman before and I'm not about to start now, but still, my blood is running hot and my muscles are tense.

I'm disappointed she's gone, though perhaps not surprised.

She's sheltered, clearly a virgin, and that moment of sexual tension between us must have been disturbing for her. Interesting how she displayed nothing but courage up until that point, all bravado as she challenged my threat to kill her if her father didn't swear his loyalty to me before sundown.

She can look death in the face, but the moment our chemistry lights up the night, she blushes and flees.

And there were you, almost going after her.

I shove back my chair and pace over to the stone balustrade that bounds the terrace. Leaning on my hands, I look out over the sea and take a breath, trying to calm myself the fuck down.

Yes, I did want to go after her. I wanted to continue our conversation. I wanted to hear more about her childhood and how difficult it was. About her father and why there were tears in her eyes when she realised he wasn't going to call me to save her, even though his treatment of her was terrible.

Did she love him? And if so, why? It seemed he didn't give a shit about her and the thought makes me burn with unexpected fury. It drags up old memories I'd thought long buried, of how my own father hated my mother's care of me, telling her it was making me 'weak'. After her death, he took my upbringing in hand to make me stronger. Hardening me to death and violence in the way of the families.

The torture session with a suspected mole that one of the other families had planted in our household, was the first. My father did the torturing along with his *consiglieri* and I was made to watch. If I protested or cried, or turned away, I was struck across the face. In the end, the *consiglieri* held me by the scruff of my neck, my mouth bleeding, one of my eyes swelling shut, and forced me to watch. I was twelve years old.

Before my mother lost herself, I was a boy who rescued baby birds from fallen nests in the garden, and once a kitten that I found on a riverbank, all wrapped up in a pillowcase after someone had tried to drown it. I helped Maria pick herbs from the garden for dinner, and for my mother, I picked roses. I loved my parents wholeheartedly and my favourite thing to do was go for walks on the beach with my mother.

But my father didn't allow such softness. There was

no room for mercy as the head of the family and no room for kindness. No room for care. He beat all that care and kindness out of me, leaving me little more than a killing machine.

Until that night I rescued Caterina, and discovered in myself that there were some shreds of kindness and care still there. Scraps of mercy, too.

I'd given up at that stage, thrown myself into my father's world because with my mother gone, it was the only world I knew. But Caterina made me see that parts of the boy I once was still remained, and that I could choose something different.

By then I had no love left for my father, not one iota. And I knew right from the start that if I wanted to keep those scraps of kindness and care, if I wanted to remain at least somewhat whole, he'd have to go. I'd have to end him myself, since I couldn't trust anyone else to do it. So, one night when he called me into his study to issue some order or other, I took my gun with me and shot him in the head.

And I didn't regret it. Not a single fucking shred.

Caterina has more of a conscience than I do, judging from the way her own father's betrayal cut her so deeply. She must care more than she thinks, which is obvious since she's been nothing but furious since she arrived here.

My fingers grip tightly to the stone as I remember the hurt in her eyes as it sunk in that her father hadn't contacted me, and my anger burns hotter at how he discarded his only daughter so carelessly.

I meant it when I told her he'd wasted an opportunity to make her his heir. She would have been the perfect head of any family, with her courage and spirit and steely determination. Her empathy too.

She was made to be a queen. She could be your *queen.*

The thought springs into my head fully formed and once it's there, it's impossible to get rid of. It's so easy to imagine her at my side, helping me to restore the Argenti family honour and to build a new empire that must come out of all this death. It feels like fate, I can't deny it, and I'm not a man who believes in fate.

The same determination I feel pursuing my cause, I see in her eyes when she's challenging me, and I can't help thinking about what we could achieve together. I've yet to meet a woman as stubborn and determined as she is.

She wants freedom, though.

Yes, but there's freedom to be had with me, as my wife. Not the freedom she's possibly imagining, but it's still freedom. And not only that, but power for the taking.

She could be your wife in every way...

That too. In fact, I can see her right now in my bed, all that raging fury turned to passion and all unleashed on me. I would take it and give her back the same, and now all I can see is her on her back, in my bed, her black hair spread out over the pillows, all that delicious golden skin laid bare, and her green eyes glittering with fire as she looks up at me. She's a woman made for physical pleasure, for screaming my name when she comes.

Fuck. I should not be thinking of her like that, because if it's sex I need, I can get that whenever I want. Yes, I made a promise to Caterina tonight, but I could bring Annika here tomorrow. Perhaps a night with her would be just what I need…

Except I don't need the wolf in me to tell me that Annika is not what I want. Any other woman is not what I want, at least not now. Not tonight.

Tonight, I want her.

I grit my teeth, staring at the darkening horizon. She was always going to be my wife in every way at some point, so why not start the seduction now? We have chemistry and I know she wants me. Yes, I didn't have the patience for a seduction earlier, but I can be patient when I want to be. After all, it took me five long years of convincing my father I was his minion completely, before I ended him with a single bullet.

It wouldn't take that long to seduce my little *gattina.* She's too passionate to hold out forever and if she needs more convincing, I can sweeten the deal. If she surrenders to me, I'll give her all the freedom and power she desires.

I think on this as the evening lengthens and I have my wedding dinner alone on the terrace. I tell Maria to take a tray up to Caterina's room, because I can't have my new wife going hungry. After that's done, I retire to my study to consider my next move. There will have to be a response to Salvatore's silence and it needs to be swift. An example will need to be made, because if there's one thing my demon of a father did get right, it's that you can't afford to be weak in this world. Not if you want to survive.

For a moment I debate the manner of Salvatore's death. I keep seeing the pain in Caterina's eyes and the faint gleam of tears when she realised her father wasn't going to save her, and the idea of putting a bullet between his eyes is a pleasurable one. He didn't deserve the daughter he ignored, but his loss will be my gain. He threw away a diamond and I will pick it up and make it the jewel in my crown.

Perhaps though, I won't kill him immediately. Perhaps I'll ask her if she has a preference. It seems right that she should choose since he took all her choices from her.

It takes me some time to put my plans in place, and it's late by the time I finish up.

I resolve to mention the question of Giovanni Salvatore's continued survival tomorrow, since my new bride will be sleeping right now, so I take a glass of brandy out onto the terrace to enjoy the night. It's a rare moment of peace, standing out in the darkness, watching the stars and listening to the waves crash on the beach below.

It reminds me of those walks on the beach with my mother, looking for sea glass and shells, and sand-smoothed stones. She loved the beach. It was the place she'd go to be free of my father, or at least to have the illusion of freedom. We'd sit together on the sand and I'd pretend to be a pirate coming to rescue her in my pirate ship, and then we'd talk about all the places we'd sail to.

I loved those moments with her. But after her third miscarriage, my father moved on to another woman, and Elena took to her bedroom in the afternoons instead of walking by the sea with me. Another thing he took from me.

The darkness is scented with sea and rosemary, and I finish my brandy. I'm about to go inside when a movement catches my eye. It's coming from the pool area, a few steps down onto another terrace from here, so I move over to the stone parapet to see what's going on.

The pool area is floodlit and a woman in a sequinned green dress is standing down one end of the pool. She has her back to me, her long black hair falling almost to her waist.

It appears that my little *gattina* is not sleeping after all.

As I watch, she reaches around to tug down the zip of her dress, before wriggling out of it. Underneath she's wearing a pair of purple silk knickers and a black sports bra, and the mismatch makes me smile. Our wedding night and she's wearing a sports bra. That seems very…her.

She discards the dress on one of the sun loungers, then, moving to the pool's edge, she dives straight in, clean and precise as a knife.

I should tell her I'm here, not stand in the darkness watching like a voyeur, but I say nothing nor do I move away. I want to watch what she'll do when she thinks she's alone, because whatever it is, I think I'll like it.

She surfaces, her hair flowing out behind her like

kelp, her body pale beneath the water. There's an elegance to her, precise lines with the most luscious curves, and in my head I'm already stripping away the bra and the knickers, so she's swimming for me naked.

Beautiful. Sheer fucking perfection.

I lean against the parapet, watching her as she begins to swim lazily to the other end of the pool before rolling onto her back and floating like a starfish. She closes her eyes, her hair moving lazily around her head. The purple silk knickers are lacy, giving me tantalising glimpses of the dark curls between her thighs, and all the blood in my veins rushes below my belt and straight to my cock.

I've seen plenty of women swimming and some more naked than she is, and never once have I had an inappropriate hard-on for any of them. But she's different. She's my wife, my little *gattina,* my queen. And right now I want her more than anything I've ever wanted in my entire life.

'I know you're there,' she says, her eyes still closed. 'If you're going to watch me at least have the decency to come out and be a man about it.'

CHAPTER ELEVEN

Caterina

I KNEW SOMEONE was watching me the moment I dove into the pool.

After the abortive dinner, I wanted to go to bed and sleep for a thousand years, and not have to think about anything, especially not Vincenzo Argenti.

But of course, it was too early for sleep and hunger kept me up. Maria left me a tray of food, including another glass of wine, and there wasn't any reason not to eat it so I did. I drank the wine too, since why not? My father left me to die and getting tipsy seemed the least of my problems.

Except, I still wasn't tired, and I was hot, and from my bedroom window I could see the pool. It looked so inviting. I didn't want to hunt around for a swimsuit in that wardrobe full of clothes, bought for a woman who isn't me, and since there appeared to be no armed guards directly near the pool, I went straight there and unzipped my dress. It was only once I was in the water that I felt someone's gaze on me.

I should have been afraid, I suppose, but I knew it

couldn't be an intruder since the security at the villa is insane. Which meant it could only be one of the guards and if so, then I wanted him to know that I knew he was there.

The water is cool on my skin and it feels wonderful to float in it weightless, with my eyes closed, free in the darkness. We had a small pool at our house in Rome and I spent a lot of time in it. Floating in the water with my eyes shut was the closest I ever got to actually feeling free, with no expectations pulling me under, nothing tying me down.

But here someone is watching, disturbing my peace, and I don't like it.

I stay in the water with my eyes closed, hoping whoever it is flees in shame, but instead I hear footsteps coming down the stone stairs from the terrace. Unhurried footsteps. Whoever it is, is not at all bothered by the fact that I spotted them.

I keep my eyes firmly shut, showing them I don't care who it is, and I'm not bothered either, but I keep listening until the footsteps come to one end of the pool and stop.

'I should call you *sirena* instead of *gattina,*' a deep, dark male voice says. 'Since you're floating in the water like a mermaid.'

Every muscle in my body tenses, my heartbeat accelerating, and I stop floating, opening my eyes to see Vincenzo Argenti standing down one end of the pool, his arms folded across his broad chest, his silver-grey gaze resting on me.

'What are you doing here?' I demand without thinking.

'I live here,' he says, infuriatingly. 'Where else would I be?'

I experience the ridiculous urge to splash him, get water all over his perfectly tailored black clothes, but that would be childish and I'm not a child, not anymore. 'I mean, why were you watching me?' I glare at him furiously. 'It's creepy.'

He lifts one shoulder, unbothered by the accusation. 'I saw some movement by the pool area so I came to investigate. I didn't want to disturb your swim.'

'And you thought watching me from the safety of a bush was better?'

His expression remains neutral. 'I wanted to make sure you didn't drown.'

Something is in the air between us again, that electricity, that tension. The one that made me leave the dinner table so quickly just before, that makes my mouth dry and my skin tight. In the cool water my nipples are hardening and I'm very aware of a nagging, throbbing ache between my thighs.

I can't pretend I don't know what it is, not now. I know exactly what it is.

You want him.

I do. I don't understand how or why, but the fact remains that I do.

He doesn't move, but his gaze moves over me and there's something in it that makes my breath catch. Something hot. I should feel vulnerable here in the water wearing only my underwear, while he's standing on the side of the pool fully dressed and towering over me, yet I don't.

That glitter in his eyes is definitely heat.

He likes looking at you half-naked.

And I realise that I like him looking. It feels good to know that while my father might have thrown me away, this man likes what he sees and he wants me.

So I stare back, feeling the tension pull tight, watching the heat in his eyes build higher and higher, and he's letting me see it. He's showing it to me.

A tremor goes through me, like a small earthquake, a key turning in a lock, an understanding I wasn't ready for even a mere few hours ago. But for some reason I'm ready now.

I've been a pawn in Giovanni Salvatore's games for so long, yet in this pool, with the Wolf of Sicily watching me, I don't feel like a pawn. I don't feel like the unloved and unwanted child of an unloving man.

With him watching, I feel like a queen.

A certain power flows through me, a power I've never experienced before, and I realise something else. He's staying right where he is. He's dangerous—so dangerous—yet he's not leaping into the water to grab me. He's not doing anything at all to compel me. He's only standing on the side of the pool, watching.

I lift my hands to my wet hair, pushing it back from my face, knowing that as I do, the wet fabric of the sports bra pulls tight across my breasts. He watches me doing that too, the burn in his eyes getting brighter.

'Well,' I say husikly. 'Here I am. Undrowned.'

'I can see that. Why did you leave our dinner so suddenly?'

The water is cool, but even so, I can feel my cheeks flushing. He knows why, I can see it in his face. 'I think you know the answer already,' I say, not willing to give him the answer quite yet. Wanting to revel in my power a little longer.

He smiles, his beautiful mouth curving, all sensual heat, and my pulse starts to race. 'Come now, *gattina.* Surely you can say it aloud?'

I've never been attracted to anyone before, still less a man like him, and naturally, sex was never a topic of conversation. So I have no experience, none at all. But along with that power, another feeling threads through me, as if a heavy weight is lifting. I'm here in the pool, married to this incredibly dangerous, beautiful man. My father has chosen his pride over me, which makes me officially free of him. I don't have to be a good Salvatore daughter anymore. I don't have to be obedient and quiet, only to be seen and not heard.

Right now, right here, I'm not free—or at least not free the way I want to be—but I'm not bound by my name. I have a different one now. I'm Caterina Argenti, and I can be whoever I want to be.

'Perhaps I don't want to say it first,' I murmur, a heady little thrill going through me as I realise that I'm flirting with him. 'Perhaps I want you to say it.'

The smile that plays around his mouth is intoxicating, as are the silver sparks glittering in his eyes. 'If you come closer, I can show you instead.'

Oh yes, definitely we're flirting, and it's one hell

of a rush. Maybe it's the champagne, or maybe it's the relentless pull of his charisma, but I can't help moving slowly through the water towards him, coming closer.

He crouches gracefully at the side of the pool, watching me as my pulse thumps in my head. I'm not afraid, even though this man has stalked my nightmares for years. Even though he kidnapped me and forced me to marry him.

He's not a nightmare anymore. He's a fever dream.

I stop at the edge of the pool, looking up at him. 'Well? I'm here. Show me then.'

For a minute he's still, then he reaches to gently grip my jaw in his strong fingers, lifting my chin. The pressure of his fingertips sends hot little sparks of electricity streaking through me, and in some dim corner of my brain, a part of me shouts a warning. This man is dangerous in ways I can't begin to comprehend, so should I be getting so close to him? Should I let him touch me like this?

But I ignore the warnings, choosing instead to look up into his eyes and seeing the heat there, bright flames of desire, and knowing that I'm the one doing this to him. I'm the one making him want.

'Are you ready?' he asks, still playing the game.

But I'm sick of games, so I put my hands on the side of the pool and push myself up, kissing him full on his beautiful, cruel mouth just as a mermaid would.

I stay there only an instant, feeling the press of his mouth on mine, the warmth and surprising softness of his lips, and I hear the sudden intake of his breath. He wasn't expecting me to do that, was he? I've shocked him, and a surge of adrenaline goes through me.

I push myself back, coming down into the water, moving slowly away, watching him, wanting to see what I did to him.

Perhaps I'm not quite done with proving my power over him after all.

He's still crouching by the side of the pool, motionless, and his smile is gone. His eyes blaze like a magnesium flare, and the raw heat in them is the most intoxicating thing I've ever seen.

'What were you going to show me again?' I ask, taunting him, my voice breathless.

'*Gattina.*' There's a rough note in the word. 'You are very naughty.'

'It's true.' I lift my hands to my hair once again, and give a sensual little stretch. 'I was the despair of my father.'

'Come here,' the Wolf orders softly. 'Or perhaps I'll come there.'

Oh, he's even more dangerous now, issuing orders like he means me to obey them. But I like it. It feels as if I'm playing with a tiger and at any moment he'll turn from a house cat into a predator, and there won't be anything I can do to stop it. It's exhilarating. I can't remember the last time I felt so like…myself.

'You won't,' I tell him, goading. 'You'll spoil all those expensive clothes.'

He rises from his crouch to his full height, all lithe, muscled grace. 'Perhaps I won't,' he agrees. 'I don't chase women as a rule and I never chase them in a pool.'

But he's not going to leave and a deep, feminine part of me knows that. It's his turn to exert his power, and I'm not immune to it. But it's my move now, and I want him to come to me. I want him to chase me. So I do the most logical thing I can think of, and pull the sports bra off over the top of my head, throwing it over the side of the pool where it lands with a wet slap against the stones.

'Suit yourself.' I reach down and slide my purple knickers off, too. 'Because I'm not getting out.' I lift the bundle of wet fabric and send them over to join the bra. 'And I like privacy when I'm swimming naked.'

The water moves like cool silk over my bare skin, but his gaze is hot and getting hotter as he sees all of me beneath the water. I can see him too, or rather the effect I'm having on him, the long, thick outline of his cock pressing against the fly of his trousers. He's not bothering to hide it either.

'Are you sure you want to keep playing this game?' he asks softly. 'Because I'm considering taking my wedding night right now, right here.'

My mouth is dry and for a moment all I can see is him diving into the pool and catching me in his arms, pushing me against the rough stone side, his mouth on mine as he pushes the hard length of his cock into me.

Desire catches me by the throat and I'm breathless. I want that. I want that *now.*

'What's stopping you then?' I ask, my voice only shaking a little. 'Can't swim?'

He doesn't speak, staring at me. Then, pausing only a moment to get rid of his shoes and socks, he dives headfirst into the pool.

Triumph surges through me. I made him come to me. I made him chase me. But it lasts only a second, because he's surfacing right in front of me, his palms already on my bare hips as he pulls me against him. His hands are hot even under the water, but not as hot as his mouth as it descends on mine.

I tremble as his tongue sweeps inside my mouth, kissing me like he owns me, and in that second he does. He owns me completely. His kiss tastes of darkness and brandy, and it's demanding. I've never experienced anything like it. I don't know what I'm doing, but something inside me is rising, something hungry and hot, and before I understand what it is, I'm kissing him back, just as demanding as he is. He adjusts his grip, one hand on my hip, the other pushing into my hair and closing his fingers into a fist, pulling my head back so he can deepen the kiss. He gives no quarter, no mercy, ravaging me like the wolf he is.

I love the dark alcoholic taste of him, along with something rich and masculine that is all his own. It makes me feel like a starving animal, and I'm pressing myself against his hard, hot body before I know what I'm doing.

He growls deep in his throat and all at once, rough stone is at my back as he pushes me against the side of the pool. Then just as I imagined it, he lifts me, wrapping my legs around his waist. I'm panting, my fingers digging into his shoulders as he feasts on my mouth, one hand beneath the water as he jerks at the buttons of his trousers.

There's nothing but demand in both of us, but even so, when the blunt head of his cock pushes into me, I have to bite down on a cry of pain. He's big, much bigger than I thought a man would be, and he's pushing relentlessly inside me. His kiss is all heat and hunger and teeth, and I'm shivering as I take him. It hurts, but I don't want him to stop, so I curl my legs tighter around him, my nails digging into the wet cotton of his shirt.

Then he's moving and the pain fades, something else replaces it. Hot, liquid pleasure. I shake even harder as he thrusts, deeper, harder, and it's not enough. I want more. I want to take him the way he's taking me, rough and hard. I want to sink my nails into his back, leave scratches on him the way I know I'll have scratches on my back from the stone side of the pool.

I growl into his mouth and he laughs, then his teeth are sinking into my bottom lip, the sharp pain adding to the building pleasure.

'Little wolf,' he murmurs against my throat, his breath warm on my skin. 'That's what you are. Not a cat. A wolf.' Then his teeth close on the delicate cords of my neck in a sharp nip, and I jerk in his grip. He thrusts deep at the same time, and I feel myself begin to come apart.

He snakes one hand down between us, to my clit and then he brushes it lightly and I scream against his mouth as the tight knot of pleasure explodes, making me fall apart completely in his arms. Barely aware of his rough growl as he follows me.

CHAPTER TWELVE

Vincenzo

THE ORGASM THAT hits me is the most intense I've experienced in years—if ever—and for long moments afterwards, all I can do is simply hold Caterina against the side of the pool, my mind blank, mainly with astonishment at myself.

I was supposed to seduce her slowly and with patience, not dive into the water because I couldn't wait, not to mention shoving her up against the side of the pool and taking her roughly. I've never lost control with a woman. Not ever.

But…the way she knew I was there, watching her, even though I was sure I hadn't betrayed myself, had delighted me. She drew me irresistibly to her like a siren on a rock. Pale and lovely in the water with her hair smooth and silky and wet down her back. Her thick black lashes were jewelled with water drops that made her eyes look like sea emeralds, and even though I should have walked away, I didn't. I couldn't.

I wanted to confront her with the reason she left our dinner, to make sure she knew that our attraction was mutual, and when she swam to the side of the pool, her green eyes dark and challenging, I'd only intended to give her a brief kiss, the start of my seduction. Yet I hadn't expected her to be the one to kiss me then swim away, as if this was a game we were playing.

I don't chase women, but I ended up chasing her, because that kiss lit a spark inside me and that spark became a blaze that threatened to consume me whole. I almost dove into the water there and then, but I managed to restrain myself. I wasn't going to dive fully dressed into a pool simply because I wanted one pretty woman.

You goaded her into taking her underwear off.

Yes, I did. But my conscience wasn't working all that well and I wanted to see how far I could push her. How far she would let herself be pushed. She wanted me, I knew that, and it became obvious the moment she took off her bra and knickers, her pale body completely naked beneath the water.

So fucking beautiful. I should have needed more of a push than what she gave me, daring me to swim after her, but it turned out that I didn't. I was barely conscious of anything beyond my own need as I dove into the water, reaching for her and pulling her into my arms. Then she was wet and slippery and her mouth was hot and sweet, and I lost all sense of myself.

There was only her, the soft press of her breasts against my chest and the silk of her hair in my fist, her sweetness on my tongue. I'd had her up against the side of the pool before I knew what I was doing and then the first press inside her… She was hot and tight, and the movement of her hips against mine drove me mad. Then the taste of her as she came, her little screams and growls, the pressure of her thighs clenching around my waist…

You hurt her.

Cold snakes through my post-orgasmic haze. I… think I did, yes. She cried out and tensed, and of course she would, because she's a good, virginal daughter of the families.

I've hurt a good many people in my time, and not felt one flicker of regret, yet the thought of hurting her…

I look down at her dark head resting against my shoulder. She's shivering.

'Caterina.' I cup her chin, tilting her head back so I can look into her eyes. 'Are you all right?'

Her gaze is dark, the brilliant green muted, yet her cheeks are flushed and her mouth looks full and swollen from my kiss. She's so beautifully wrecked by me, I want to growl with satisfaction.

'Yes,' she says, sounding dazed.

'I hurt you.'

'Only for a moment.' She winces. 'My back is sore, though.'

I tug her forward and that's when I see the scrapes down her spine from where I pressed her against the stone side of the pool. And a curiously sharp burst of anger goes through me, at myself and my fucking lack of control. Because I know what happens when I lose it; people tend to die.

You also had sex with her without a condom.

That should make the situation a thousand times worse, yet even as my anger smoulders, a part of me, the wolf, is pleased that I've claimed her for himself. Pleased at the prospect of a child.

It's a primitive thought and one I shouldn't embrace, yet everything in me embraces it all the same. She's mine now. Mine in *every* way, and there can be no letting her go. She'll remain my wife, rule at my side, and bear my children. This will be a marriage in every way there is.

But will that be what she wants?

I don't like the murmurs of my conscience and ignore it as I get us both out of the pool. There are towels on all the sun loungers, so I sit her down on one and start drying her, being careful with the scratches on her back.

She shivers deliciously as I touch her, gazing at me from beneath thick black lashes. 'You look very serious all of a sudden,' she murmurs. 'Was it that bad?'

I'm kneeling on the stone pavers in front of her and the instant after she says the words I grip her chin firmly in my hand and force her to look at me. 'That wasn't bad,' I say, suddenly ferocious. 'That was fucking poetry.'

She blinks, searching my face as if she doesn't quite believe me. 'Oh...' Colour flushes her cheeks. '*Oh*... well. I have nothing to compare it to and I thought that look on your face meant—'

'That look on my face means I've decided you're my wife in every way there is,' I interrupt, forceful now. 'You'll be in my bed every night and once all the families are united, we'll rule over them together. You'll be the mother of my children and—'

'Absolutely the fuck not.' Her ready temper ignites, green and gold sparks glittering in her eyes. 'Are you insane?'

I grip her tighter. I will not be denied, not on this. 'I'm not. Why do you think I married you?'

But her gaze doesn't even flicker. 'To get my father's loyalty. At least that's what you told me.'

'*Gattina.*' I struggle to keep a grip on my temper, since getting angry with her will only make things worse. 'It was always going to be a real marriage at some point, surely you must know that?'

She has no such qualms. 'How would I know?' she demands. 'You didn't tell me what else you were intending beyond having sex with your mistress tonight.'

Ah, *Dio.* She's not going to let me get away with anything, is she?

'Well, I'm telling you now,' I say, refusing to feel any shame about the fact that I wasn't exactly clear when I kidnapped her. 'That's what I intend.'

'In that case, no.' She jerks her chin from my fingers. 'I want freedom, Vincenzo Argenti, not another cage.'

My grip on my temper slips and it flares in response to hers. This isn't going the way I want it to, and I have a feeling that it's my fault.

Of course it's your fault. You're treating her like an object again. The way your father treated your mother.

This time I can't ignore the thought, or the shame that comes with it. I swore to be a better man than that bastard Stefano, and yet here I am, doing exactly what he did to my mother, railroading her, ignoring her wishes in favour of my own. I'm a man who learns from his mistakes and I should be learning from this one.

So I don't move, still looking into her face as I force my temper into submission. 'You think marriage to me would be a cage? Why?'

'Why do you think?' That stubborn little chin of hers juts. 'I'll be relegated to sidelines. Not allowed to do anything but bear children and support my husband for "safety's" sake. Being the little woman looking after the home. That's a cage however you look at it.'

She's right. You know she's right.

I grit my teeth, forcing away the urgent need to press her back against the sun lounger cushion and show her exactly how good this 'cage' can make her feel. 'Then what does freedom look like to you?' I try to make the words sound less reluctant, but no doubt I fail.

She gazes back, all challenge. 'Are you asking me that because you think I need to hear it or because you actually want to know?'

Goddamn. Why had I ever thought this woman would make a good and biddable wife? When she opposes me at every turn? But oddly, when I force myself to think about it, I discover that I actually *do* want to know.

'Tell me,' I growl, getting annoyed with myself now.

Her expression is furious at first, but then that fades, and she glances down at her knees. 'I only want a normal life,' she says, her voice softening. 'I want to have a career and get a flat, have some friends. Maybe have a boyfriend and a cat.' She pauses and then lifts her gaze to mine. 'I don't want to be told what to do anymore. I don't want to be forced into a box I don't fit and never have. I don't want to be surrounded all day every day by guards. I don't want to have to fear for my own life or those of any children I have someday. And I don't want to feel as if…' Another little pause and then she forces herself to go on. 'I don't want to feel like the unloved and unwanted child my father was stuck with after my mother and brother died.'

She's got an uncanny aim when she throws those spears of hers. They always land directly in my chest, the tips brushing up against my heart, hurting.

Unloved. Unwanted. Those words resonate in a way I don't like at all.

That was how my mother felt just before she died, and I know because she told me one night as the sedatives were kicking in. That's how I felt too, when my father struck me across the face for refusing to look at a torture session. He didn't care about me. He only cared about himself and how much I shamed him.

Elena didn't care about you either.

A sullen anger sits in my gut, an anger I don't want to acknowledge. For how my mother withdrew from me, slowly but surely retreating into herself. Nothing I did made any difference. She might not have left me physically, but she left me emotionally, and she never came back.

But then love does that to a person. It kills them

slowly and by degrees, and so before it killed me, I cut it from my soul just like my father cut it away from my mother. He killed her love for him and so I killed mine for both of them, and I never regretted it.

Except I know that love hasn't died for Caterina. I saw it in her tears at dinner just before, the grief that her father hadn't come for her. Grief comes from love, and so no matter how awful her father was, she still feels some kind of love for him.

'You are not unwanted,' I say. 'Know that right now. But love will not be part of our marriage, not ever.'

Surprise flickers across her face. 'I didn't say anything about love.'

'You did. You said you didn't want to feel unloved and unwanted.'

'I didn't mean loved by you,' she snaps back, her anger returning.

'Good.' I ignore what surely can't be a kick of disappointment.

'I was talking about freedom,' Caterina says insistently. 'And love doesn't mean freedom, so why should I want that anyway?'

I narrow my gaze, searching her expression, because this talk of love, when I've only known her an afternoon and evening, is far too premature. 'Forget love,' I say, dismissive. 'I can offer you certain freedoms, but you must understand that your life will be curtailed to some extent purely because you're married to me.'

This does not mollify her. Unsurprisingly.

'You can see why I didn't want to get married,

right? But, oh wait, you didn't care about what I wanted, did you?'

Her sarcastic wit amused me before, but it's not amusing me now. It's hitting me in places I thought were well defended and I don't like it one bit.

I rise to my feet, dropping the towel onto the cushions beside her, before getting rid of my wet clothes. Then I hold out my hand. 'Come, *gattina,*' I order peremptorily. 'This conversation is over. It's time for bed.'

CHAPTER THIRTEEN

Caterina

I'M SITTING ON the sun lounger naked, with him towering over me. His hand is extended as if I'm one of his mindless soldiers, ready to obey his every command, and a part of me is actually desperate to obey this command at least.

Because he's beautiful, like a sculpture of an ancient god beaten out of bronze. Every muscle is sharply delineated, the ridged plane of his stomach and the powerful length of his thighs making my mouth go dry. That and his cock, long and thick, and already getting hard.

I've never seen a naked man before in the flesh and while he's gorgeous, I still don't want to give in no matter how beautiful he is. His will is as strong as mine, and I know that if I give him an inch, he'll take a mile, and there's no way I'm going to do that. Not when he's taken so many miles already and so quickly.

I shouldn't have been so honest about what I didn't want, but it slipped out before I could think. His stroking hand was soothing as he dried me off and the warmth of his naked body was so close to mine, I felt almost relaxed. Especially after that incredible orgasm. And naturally I said something I shouldn't, and his reaction…

He'd been so very emphatic about what our marriage would be and then about love, and yes, that had made me angry. Firstly, I'd never wanted to be married at all, let alone to him, and at no point did I agree to any of the nonsense he said about children and ruling at his side. Secondly, I don't know why me saying I didn't want to be unloved and unwanted had made him suddenly go off about not wanting love in our marriage. I hardly know him, let alone love him, and he's not the kind of man I want to fall in love with anyway. He may be hot, but he's everything I *don't* want, no matter how many orgasms he gives me.

You really liked that orgasm, though.

I push the thought away hard. I may know nothing about sex, but an orgasm doesn't mean love, and this is about more than sex anyway. I don't want a man telling me what to do again. I refuse. I won't be his trophy wife, safely locked away behind glass, and I won't be his brood mare, giving him a child whenever he asks.

So, I ignore his outstretched hand, get up off the sun lounger, and walk straight past him, over to where I dumped my underwear. I wring them out then pick them up, before heading to where I left my green dress, and pick that up too. All the while ignoring him completely. Tossing the green dress over my shoulder, I turn my back on him and start walking up the stairs to the villa.

'Caterina,' he says, impatiently.

I keep walking.

'Stop, Caterina.' His voice is harder this time.

But I don't stop.

'*Caterina!*' he roars as I reach the top of the steps.

Again, I ignore him, trying to walk sedately to the villa so he can't tell how furious I am. But my walk has turned into a stalk, so he'll probably guess anyway. My skin prickles and my heart begins to race as I feel his gaze boring into my back, and part of me clenches in anticipation. It wants him to chase me again, catch me again, lose control again, fall apart with me again, because it felt so good and so powerful.

But I don't hear footsteps and the only thing I feel are those prickles, not his hot hands, and the part of me that wanted him is bitterly disappointed.

I push that feeling away too, as I stalk naked past the guards, all studiously looking the other way, because no, I'm not disappointed. He gave me my first taste of sex, and while it was good, I'm sure it's not as good as he said it was.

'*That was fucking poetry...*'

A shiver goes down my spine and something aches inside me, a longing I don't want to feel. His gaze had burned when he'd told me that, gripping my jaw tightly, as if it was important that I understand. And he meant it, I could tell. The way he came after me, the way he kissed me, the way he held me, as if he was starving for me, that was all real.

'*You are not unwanted.*'

I don't want that to touch me, but it does. Since my

mother died, I've never felt wanted by anyone, and my father giving up my life as if it meant nothing to him felt like yet more confirmation of my worthlessness. Yet the Wolf wanted me, and that healed a small part of my soul.

But then he'd gone and spoiled it all by raving about ruling with him and children, and having my freedom curtailed, and how love will never be part of our marriage.

You shouldn't have walked off. You should have stayed and made him discuss it.

How could I? When he'd been very clear he didn't want to talk about it?

I go upstairs and slam the bedroom door hard to get that snide thought out of my head, then I go into the bathroom. Dumping the wet clothes in the vanity sink, I then turn on the water in the huge white marble walk-in shower, and stand under the flow. The heat loosens my muscles, but it doesn't do anything for my fury.

You kind of did this to yourself. If you were the good little girl your father wanted you to be, maybe it wouldn't be so difficult.

I squeeze some shower gel onto my skin and angrily wash myself, even as the truth sits, sharp and cold as ice in the pit of my stomach. Perhaps it's true. Perhaps if I'd been the compliant child Dad wanted, none of this would be a problem. I'd be as happy to be Carlo's wife as I would to be Vincenzo Argenti's, wanting nothing more than to raise children, manage a household, and sit gossiping with the other *cosa nos-*

tra wives. I'd be blind to the bars of the cage. It would only be a villa, protected by guards, nothing more.

Maybe your father was right. None of this would be a problem if you'd died along with your mother and Alessio.

My throat closes, but I swallow hard, refusing to acknowledge the pain that thought brings with it. Plenty of times I'd wished the Wolf hadn't saved me, that Mama or Alessio had been saved instead. If they had, maybe my father would have been kinder, happier… But there's no point thinking about all of that, because that's not what happened. I lived and my father never got over it.

I turn off the water and dry myself, before walking into the bedroom.

I'm suddenly exhausted and it's very late, and now my anger is ebbing, I'm inexplicably on the verge of tears. I need to go to bed and forget about the Wolf and my father for a few hours, and hopefully dream of nothing.

There's only diaphanous, silky nightgowns that are almost transparent in the drawers, so I settle for a new pair of knickers and a T-shirt to wear to bed. And I'm just about to slide under the covers when a note is pushed under my door. I scowl at it for a bit, because no prizes for guessing who pushed it there, but eventually I pick it up. Maybe it's an apology and a good faith offer to give me a new identity and a new life far away from here.

But of course it isn't.

On the white paper, words are scrawled in forceful blank ink: *How would you like your father to die?*

The Wolf is making his move and he's going punish my father for his lack of response. I pretty much expected he would, but I'm shocked that firstly, he's asking me for a method, and secondly, that my instant response is that I don't want my father to die.

He's a terrible father, but I won't stoop to his level. He left me to die without any apparent qualms, but I'm not the same as he is. The Wolf told me I wasn't a killer, and he's right, I'm not. I won't sacrifice a life for pettiness' sake, even the life of a man who doesn't deserve the chance I'm giving him.

I pick up the piece of paper, find a pen in the bedside table drawer, and scrawl on the back: *Don't you dare kill him. I'm not stooping to his level and letting him be murdered because I don't like him. He can live and be alone for the rest of his life.*

Then I shove the piece of paper back under the door.

CHAPTER FOURTEEN

Vincenzo

I'm in a terrible mood the next morning. I slept badly after Caterina left me standing by the pool, which is not helping, but mainly I'm furious with myself for letting a beautiful, green-eyed banshee get under my skin so badly.

My terrible sleep is her fault entirely. I kept dreaming of diving into pools and reaching for her, only to feel her slippery-smooth body slide out of my hands, over and over again.

That's not her fault. That's yours.

It's a truth that I don't want to acknowledge, yet it burns a hole in my brain all the same. I'd dismissed the conversation because I didn't like the direction it was going, and besides, I was getting hard for her again and wanted her in my bed.

But, of course, my beautiful, oppositional little wife wasn't having a bar of that. She didn't explain when she got to her feet and walked proudly past my outstretched hand. Then again, she didn't need to. I could see the flames in her eyes.

She had a right to be angry.

I didn't handle announcing my intentions to her very well, that's true. I could have worded my statements slightly differently, to make them sound less like proclamations and more like suggestions. An offer of a discussion would have probably been more welcome. After all, I'm trying not to be like my father. Yes, 'trying' being the operative word.

Still, what I'm asking of her wouldn't have been any different to what the Bianchi boy would have asked, so why she got so furious is anyone's guess.

Your dismissal of love, then of the whole conversation, might have had something to do with it.

That particular thought is an uncomfortable one, particularly when I remember what she said about being unloved and unwanted. That had been an unexpected confession and there'd been pain in her eyes when she'd said it, which had made me angry. I'd tried not to be, but in retrospect, I failed badly and been dismissive instead.

She didn't need your anger. She needed your understanding.

I stalk grimly into my office with an espresso, the whispers of my long-dead conscience needling at me. I'm not used to considering other people or even understanding them, because neither consideration nor understanding affects my decisions. Their feelings don't matter in the greater scheme of things, so why I keep thinking about Caterina Salvatore's is anyone's guess.

I down my espresso in one go then sit down at my desk. I have work to do and many things to arrange, and I can't afford to be sitting here thinking about my new wife for hours on end. Yet on the desk in front of me lies the piece of paper she wrote her angry reply on, and it's impossible to think of anything else.

She's relentless in her opposition, even demanding I not issue a hit on her father, because she wants him to live. However, while I understand her qualms and have long let go wanting to avenge my mother's death, I'm still furious at him for his treatment of her. Everything in me is telling me that I need to make an example of him, yet I can't stop reading the words on her note.

I'm not stooping to his level...

She might not stoop, but I've done so many times, and while I see the irony of fighting violence with violence, as I've always believed, the ends justifies the means.

She's not thinking that, though, and now she's got me second-guessing. She doesn't want to be her father—that's what she said in the note—and like her, I don't want to be mine. Yet if I kill Giovanni Salvatore, how am I any different?

Stefano ordered the death of the Salvatore family because of the offence against our family's honour when my mother died. And in killing Giovanni, I'll be doing the same thing. I always thought that allowable, because I'd be taking out our last enemy, and besides it would end with me. Yet…

What if you didn't? What if it ended with Giovanni instead?

No, I can't start thinking like her. I have to take him out or get his loyalty, that's vital to my plans of unification, and there can be no middle ground. There never is in the families.

So why am I still hesitating? Why am I thinking about letting him live? Just because she wants me to?

I'm in the middle of puzzling through this when my door bursts open and Caterina enters the room. She's in a flowing dress the colour of sunflowers and she looks like a ray of sunshine come streaming into my office. But not her eyes. They're sharp chips of emerald mined from the dark side of the moon.

'If you've ordered his death,' she announces without preamble, 'I'll kill you myself.'

The kick of heat that goes through me at the sight of her is a drug and I can't get enough. I want to leap straight over my desk and grab her, devour her, but I can't allow that. I lost control badly last night and it's not going to happen again, so I lean back in my chair and let her fury wash over me instead.

'You have feelings about it, I gather.' I push out my chair and put one foot on the opposite knee. 'At least, judging by that note and your latest threat to my person.'

When people stand before my desk, they're usually white with fear, but not my Caterina. She storms up to the desk itself, puts her hands on the edge and leans forward. Her hair slides over her shoulders, brushing the desktop and the neckline of her dress dips, making it very clear that she's not wearing a bra.

'Damn right, I have feelings,' she says, staring daggers at me. 'He's a terrible father, but that doesn't mean I want him to die. No one should have the power to make life-and-death decisions about another human being.'

Ah, now we're getting into it. Pity. I have no patience for conversations about ethics. 'And yet people make those decisions every day,' I say, trying to keep my gaze from the neckline of her dress. 'Anyway, it's not your decision. It's mine.'

'He's *my* father,' she insists. 'Who decided you get to be judge, jury and executioner anyway?'

It's difficult to concentrate on what she's talking about, especially when she clearly has no concept of what I can see and the fact that I'm already starting to get hard. 'What do you care?' I demand, losing patience. 'I'll be the one taking his life, not you.'

She takes a breath, fury still burning in her eyes. 'Because I'll know I could have stopped you.'

'Oh yes?' I hold her gaze, letting her see what she's up against, the absolute force of my will. 'And how could you have done that, *gattina*?'

At first she's still, just staring at me. Then she takes another breath, pushes herself away from the desk and straightens up. Then before I can move or speak, she's coming around to where I'm sitting and sliding herself up onto the desk in front of me. Then she daintily places one elegant, bare foot on each of the arms of my chair and grips the hem of her dress. 'Let him live and I'll let you do whatever you want with me, Wolf.'

A wolf is what I am and a starving one at that, because I can see a little way up her dress, as she no doubt intended, to the soft, pale skin of her inner thighs, and I can smell in the air the scent of jasmine and aroused woman.

She's using sex against me, and why shouldn't she? After what happened between us last night? I'd admire her guts if I didn't want her so fucking much.

It shouldn't be difficult to refuse, it shouldn't, because this matters to me. This matters to my cause. I can't be seen to be weak, not at this time, and that's exactly what letting Salvatore live would make me seem.

But it *is* difficult to refuse. Because now all I can think about is shoving my chair back, stripping her dress off and laying her back on my desk to taste every inch of her.

'What makes you think I want to do anything at all with you?' I drawl, trying to fight her pull. 'Especially when I've already had you.'

She doesn't speak, but her gaze drops to my lap, where I'm already hard.

'Oh, that?' I don't move. 'I can easily get someone else to see to that. Or I could handle it myself. I have at least one working hand, after all.'

'You don't want your hand.' She's looking straight at me when she says this, as if she knows. As if she can see the truth in my gaze. 'You want me.'

Holy fuck, this woman... She's barely had sex, has no conception of men, yet she's manipulating me with the ease of a practiced flirt. And I'm letting her do it.

She's right. You want her. So take her.

The wolf in me will brook no argument and before I know what I'm doing, I'm shoving back my chair, and stepping between her parted thighs. My hands reach for her hips, feeling the warmth of her body through the thin fabric of her dress.

Her eyes widen and she puts out a hand, her palm landing directly on my chest. 'He lives,' she says insistently. 'Promise me.'

I don't want to. An example needs to be made, yet that's not what I say. 'Yes,' I say instead, barely even thinking about Salvatore and my wretched crusade, everything concentrated on the woman in front of me. 'I promise.'

Her hand slides up my chest, to the back of my head and she pulls my mouth down on hers, and I'm lost. She tastes sweet, like honey and vanilla, and I can't get enough. I devour her, my hands automatically dropping to grab fistfuls of her dress, pulling the hem up to her waist. She gasps against my mouth as I slide a hand between her thighs to find she's not wearing any underwear.

'Naughty, *gattina,*' I murmur as I find her sensitive little clit and stroke her there lightly. 'Using sex to manipulate me.'

She shivers, gasping again as I explore the soft folds between her thighs, stroking her, feeling how incredibly wet she is already for me. 'I… I'm not m-manipulating you,' she whispers. 'I'm only using whatever I can to make sure my father stays alive.'

I slide a finger inside her, then as she moans, another. She's so wet there's no resistance and I'm more than ready to replace those fingers with my cock. But I'm not going to do that now. I'm going to take my time now, explore her completely, undo her the way she's undoing me.

I lift my mouth from hers. 'I'm going to want more than one wedding night,' I say as I trail kisses down the side of her neck, moving my hand to drive her steadily mad. 'I'm going to want you in my bed every night.'

She sighs, her hips shifting against my hand so I withdraw it. 'Promise me,' I say, echoing her as I lift my head and look down into her pleasure-flushed face.

Her eyes are dark, forest green instead of grass, and her mouth is full and red from my kiss. She's delectable, all her anger transmuted into raw desire, and I can't help but think of all the arguments we're going to have and how sweet the making up will be.

'Please,' she says, her voice husky. 'Please…'

'That's not what I asked.' I reach out to cup one side of her face, my thumb tracing the full curve of her bottom lip. It feels so soft I want to bite her. I want to bite all of her, eat her alive. 'You must say "I promise, Vincenzo".'

She shivers, her gaze captured by mine as I ease my thumb between her lips and into the heat of her mouth. Her lashes drift shut as I feel the soft tip of her curious tongue against my skin, and my cock is so hard it's almost painful. But I'm not rushing this, not now, not like last night.

I take my thumb from her mouth, rubbing the pad of it over her lower lip, and her lashes flutter. 'Say it,' I order softly. 'Give me the words, *gattina*, and I'll consider making you come.'

She swallows, the pulse at the base of her throat racing as her lashes lift. 'I…p-promise,' she breathes.

'My name, Caterina,' I remind her as I grip the hem of her dress. 'I want you to say it. I want to hear it.'

She takes a shuddering breath and for a second I think she's not going to give it to me. But then she says, 'I promise, Vincenzo.'

My name sounds like a prayer in her mouth and abruptly, I can't wait any longer. Not that I need to now since I've got what I wanted.

'Lift your arms,' I say and she does, letting me pull the yellow dress up and over her head, and then off.

Beneath it she's naked and just as beautiful sitting on my desk as she was floating in my pool the night before. Her skin light olive and silky. Her breasts perfectly round with hard little pink nipples. Dark curls between her smooth thighs.

She looks up at me, utterly unselfconscious, as if daring me to find fault with her, but I can't. 'My wife, you are flawless,' I tell her. 'And now I'm going to give you what I promised you.'

Then I put my hands between her thighs and spread them wide.

CHAPTER FIFTEEN

Caterina

I'M SITTING NAKED on his desk, my body wound so tight I can hardly breathe. The feel of his big, warm hands spreading my legs wide apart is almost too much. I'm sensitised all over, my mouth throbbing from his kiss, my clit aching from the touch of his fingers, my sex wet and my nipples hard.

This morning I woke up, vividly remembering what had happened between us last night. But I didn't want to think about the sex and what it meant. I was wholly consumed with the idea that he'd ignore what I'd written about leaving my father alive, and issue a hit on him anyway.

In the cold light of day it seemed even more important that he live. No matter what kind of father he'd been to me, he was still my father and no one should get to say who lived and who died. Especially not the Wolf of Sicily.

So I decided that Vincenzo needed to understand that. I had to get a promise from him that he'd leave my father alone, another vow like the one he gave me when he said he wouldn't hurt me, and there was only one way I could think of to do that.

So I got out of bed and had a shower. Used some of the scented body lotion that was sitting on the vanity, smoothing it everywhere. Then I walked determinedly to the closet, leafing through the dresses until I found one that looked good on me, and I put it on. Without underwear.

He wanted me, I knew that. He'd dived straight into the water, still dressed, to get to me the night before and there had been no holding back from him. I'd tested the power of my sexuality on him last night and it had brought him to his knees, and that meant I could do it again.

I could use it to get him to do what I wanted, and since that was the only power I had here, why the hell shouldn't I?

Impetuous of me, but since I didn't want to think about what was going to happen beyond saving my father, I simply headed downstairs and bearded the wolf in his den.

He'd been as intimidatingly beautiful as he had been the night before, lounging there behind his desk. His silver eyes full of flames and a cynical, barbed amusement. He was in a white shirt this morning, the top buttons undone and the cuffs rolled up, and plain black suit trousers. Austere, yet also making him look devastatingly attractive.

I'd known a moment of doubt as I'd stormed over to him, leaning on his desk and making my demands, because he'd appeared so determinedly unmoved. But then I'd caught the dip of his gaze to the neckline of my dress and all my doubts vanished.

If he was so determined to take this path, he'd discover that there was at least one person more determined than he was. Me.

So I'd rounded his desk before he could move, and I pushed myself up on top of it right in front of him. And I'd placed my feet on the arms of his chair so there could be no doubt about what I was offering. Then I'd made my demands.

It had worked beautifully. He'd been up out of the chair, his hands on me before I'd had a moment to think, but I'd at least had the presence of mind to make him give me his promise before anything else happened. And I got that.

But I hadn't expected him to make demands of me in return, to be in his bed every night. There was danger there and I knew it, though with his hands on me, his mouth on mine, my brain was too fogged with desire to know where the danger came from. And when he'd put his thumb in my mouth, shocking me, then electrifying me with the taste of his skin, all I could think about was, yes, that's exactly where I wanted to be every night. In his bed.

I could have refused, I really could have. I hadn't needed to give in. But if I hadn't, I knew what would happen. He'd walk away from me, leaving me aching and wanting and furious the way I'd been last night, and I didn't think I could do that again.

And I know now as he spreads my thighs apart, his gaze fierce and hungry, that I'd been lying to myself last night. I didn't think sex could have the same power over me as it had over him, but it does. His every touch, his every look makes me feel wanted in a way I haven't felt since I was a child, not to mention free. I'd felt it in the pool last night as I'd taken my underwear off, daring him to come and get me, and I want that feeling. I want that freedom.

So, I can't feel any regrets as he kneels before me, spreading me apart with his fingers, and even if I had any, they're lost in a blaze of electric pleasure as he ducks his head between my legs and puts his mouth on me.

I cry out, my head going back, lights exploding behind my eyes. The slow stroke of his tongue everywhere but the place I want him to lick most of all is maddening. He's feasting on me, tasting me like I'm a banquet set before him, but he's not going to gorge. No, he's going to take a bite from every dish and take his time savouring the flavour.

'Look at me,' he growls in a dark, rough voice.

I can't help but obey, looking down into his fierce, quicksilver gaze as hc spcars his tongue into me. I shudder, another cry bursting from my throat. The sight of him there, with his long fingers gripping my thighs, is the mostly intensely erotic thing I've ever seen.

He licks me and nips me, exploring me, but never quite giving me what I want, and I'm panting, writhing on the desk, unable to stop from begging him. It should be humiliating to beg for anything from him, but in this moment I don't care how I sound. I just want what he promised, which was to make me come.

'Vincenzo,' I pant. 'Wolf...please...oh please.'

This time he answers, giving me the most delicate lick and caress, right on my clit, and the world explodes around me in a burst of colour and unbelievable pleasure.

The room echoes with the sounds of someone's cries, and dimly I know they're mine. I'm lying back on his desk now, shuddering with the aftershocks, in pieces yet whole at the same time.

He rises to his feet, standing between my spread thighs, arrogantly looking down at my naked body stretched out before him as he undoes his belt. He locks gazes with me, his eyes liquid mercury, and the heat in them makes me burn all over once again.

His movements are lazy as he unbuttons his trousers and pulls down the zip of his fly, but there is nothing lazy in the way he looks at me. I expect him to pull me to him, but he doesn't. Instead, like the wolf he is, he leaps gracefully up onto the desk and looms over me on his hands and knees. He's a predator about to feast on his prey, and I'm shivering with anticipation.

He leans down to take my mouth, his kiss electric, the taste of me on his lips, and I lift my hands, threading my fingers into his black hair, feeling the rough silk of it against my skin.

I arch up, wanting him, and he slides a hand beneath the small of my back, keeping me in position. Then his weight settles on me, and his hands are moving, and I feel the thick, blunt head of his cock pushing into me.

There is no pain this time, only the most incredible pleasure and he sinks deep inside me. I moan as his hand beneath my back slides further down, gripping my butt hard, and then he begins to move. It's slow at first, agonisingly so, making me gasp and moan against him. I pull at his hair, find his mouth, then nip at him, biting at him so he goes harder, faster, but frustratingly, his kisses are as slow and sensual as the movement of his hips.

His lips burns at my throat then move lower, the scattered sparks of hot kisses raining over my breasts, his tongue lazily licking at my nipples. I'm gasping again, arching against him, begging and begging, but he only gives a dark, heated laugh against my skin and carries on driving me insane.

He slides his hands up my thighs, pulling my legs up and around his lean hips, sinking even deeper inside me, and there's nothing I can do to resist the storm of pleasure building inside me. Nothing I can do but surrender to it.

So, I do, my nails digging into his powerful shoulders as he thrusts deeply, lazily into me. And only when I think I can't bear it anymore, does he ease a finger down between us, timing a stroke over my clit with a deep thrust of his cock, and I'm lost as the storm breaks over me.

Dimly I feel him move faster, harder, and then I hear the harsh growl of my name in his ear, and I grip him tighter, holding him to me as the storm breaks in him as well.

Some time passes, I don't know how long, but I'm

curiously comfortable, despite the hard wood of the desk against my back and the weight of his hard muscled body pressing down on my front. I've still got my fingers twisted in his hair, and I'm stroking it, looking at the strands of silver threading through all that ink-black. They're beautiful. As beautiful as he is.

After a moment, he lifts his head and looks down at me, his intense gaze searching mine. 'You are a revelation, little *gattina,*' he murmurs. 'I have never met a woman like you.'

He means it, I can see, and a warmth that has nothing to do with sex or physical chemistry fills me. I've never been any kind of revelation to anyone, let alone to a man like him, and I love the way he says it.

'And I've never met a man like you.' I shouldn't give him this truth, I shouldn't give him any part of me at all, and yet I find myself wanting to.

'Is that a good thing?' he asks, his voice wholly empty of the lazy, cynical amusement I'm used to hearing in it.

I stare up at him, meeting his silver gaze. 'Yes,' I say. 'It's a very good thing.'

He smiles that sexy, genuine smile of his, that turns his mouth from cruel to beautiful in seconds flat. 'Well, that's true. I am very special.'

And for the first time since I met him, my own mouth curves in response, giving him back his own smile. 'Not to mention, arrogant as hell,' I say, teasing him a little.

'That shouldn't be a surprise,' he says, his voice full of masculine satisfaction. 'I have a lot to be arrogant about.' He moves off the desk, doing his trousers back up and then, as I sit up, he scoops me up and into his arms. 'Why don't we continue this upstairs, hmmm?'

'That's the best idea I've heard from you yet,' I say as he carries me from his office.

We spend all day in his large, four-poster bed, and he shows me just how much pleasure my body is capable of. Then he lets me experiment on him, telling me what he likes, and I'm thrilled when I have him growling rough demands, before roaring my name as he comes.

But it's not until the late afternoon, when he turns in bed to take a sip of the champagne Maria brought up for us, along with some food for 'sustenance', and the sheet slips down, exposing his back. There are deep, jagged scars marring his smooth deep-olive skin. They're twisted and angry-looking, as if someone has gouged great holes his flesh, and everything in me draws tight with horror.

I must have made some kind of involuntary sound, because he puts down his champagne glass and turns back to look at me, frowning. 'What wrong?'

I'm cold all over, aware all of a sudden of where I am and exactly who he is. The Wolf of Sicily, head of the most infamous and powerful of the families. The man who's ordered hundreds of deaths and forced into submission many other families. And I'm his wife. And I'll be trapped in this cage for the rest of my life.

'Caterina,' he says my name sharp with concern. 'Are you okay?' He gently cups my cheek in his palm, and it doesn't feel like the hand of a monster or a killer. It feels warm and familiar. 'You've gone very pale.'

I don't want to be afraid of him, not now, not when I haven't been before, so I ignore the fear. Instead I say, 'Those scars on your back. What happened?'

A shadow moves in his eyes, but it's gone too fast for me to tell what it was. Then as smoothly as a key turning in a lock, the mask of the Wolf settles over his features. The face of the head of the Argenti family.

'It's not a pretty story, *gattina,*' he says lightly. 'And definitely not one to share when there are other things we could be doing.'

He's trying to distract me and if he was a different sort of man, I'd let him. But he's not a different sort of man. He is who he is and he's my husband, and I have to keep pushing so he doesn't walk all over me.

'Tell me,' I demand.

His mouth thins. He's clearly unhappy with this, but doesn't attempt another distraction. 'The scars are from a punishment my father gave me. He was from the "spare the rod and spoil the child" school of parenting. So when I didn't obey his orders, he would whip me with his studded belt.' The Wolf says the words as if they mean nothing to him, as if they aren't connected to him at all, but all I feel is cold horror.

I was punished by my father, but he never touched me. All my punishments were psychological, little criticisms here and there, death from a thousand cuts. But this...those terrible, awful, gouges... I can't imagine the pain he must have been in.

'Don't look at me like that,' the Wolf snaps suddenly, anger flickering through his eyes. 'It was a couple of strikes, nothing more. He did much worse to other people. I got off easy, believe me.'

His anger sparks mine and I say heedlessly, 'I wasn't looking at you with pity, Vincenzo. That was horror.'

He stares at me for a long moment and I don't flinch from his gaze. Then the silver flames in his eyes abruptly die away and he says in a milder tone, 'It was twenty years ago, a long time. They don't hurt anymore.'

He's trying to reassure me, I think, but I'm not in the least bit reassured. 'What had you done to deserve it?' I ask. 'Because that seems excessive.'

'If I'd been anyone else but his heir, I would have been killed.' Unexpectedly, he looks down at the white sheet covering him. 'Stefano did love his little punishments.'

'You didn't answer me.' Suddenly it seems important that I know this. 'What was it for?'

He doesn't look up. 'I think you already know what it was for.'

A wave of ice washes over me. Of course I know.

That was his punishment for letting me live.

'Vincenzo…' His name comes out hoarse, and I want to go on, but I don't know what to say. The only thing that comes to me that I'm sorry, I'm so sorry you had to bear that. I'm so sorry I was the cause. But I don't think he wants to hear that.

'No,' he says softly, a note of warning in the word. 'That part of my life is over. I ended it myself when I paid him back in kind.' Abruptly, he looks up from the white sheet, his gaze blazing into mine. 'But know this, Caterina. I never *ever* regretted saving you. Not once.'

My throat closes and there are unexpected tears in my eyes, and I have no idea why. I have no idea why my heart aches or why the thought of the pain he had to endure because of me, hurts me too. I shouldn't hurt because of what happened to him as a child, not considering all the lives he's taken and the things he's done, and yet, he doesn't seem a monster sitting here beside me in the bed.

He's only a man who was a boy, a long time ago.

'I blamed you for their deaths for years,' I tell him hoarsely, unable to stop myself. 'You were in my nightmares, always chasing me to kill me. I'm claustrophobic because I spent two days in that closet before anyone thought to check on me. I thought you were a monster.' I swallow, my throat painful. 'But I was wrong.'

More shadows chase themselves over his beautiful face. 'No,' he says softly. 'I'm still a monster, *gattina.* Don't ever think otherwise.' He lifts a hand and brushes away a tear that has escaped with a gentle fingertip. 'But you were so little. No wonder you had nightmares.'

'But those scars…' I swallow again, not sure why I'm still crying. 'What you had to endure because of me—'

'No,' he repeats, softly and yet very firmly. 'I told you. I never regretted saving you and I meant it. I mean it still.' He pauses a moment, then adds, 'You changed my life. It's because of you that I started down this road, to stop the violence. To end the killings. You were the catalyst for all of this, so how could I ever regret it?'

I don't know what to say to that and I don't know how to feel. My heart aches for him, but also for myself. Because this path I somehow sent him down, is as bloody as the path he seems to think he's avoiding. I don't want to say that, though, not now. I don't have the energy to keep pushing, and the way he's looking at me, the way he's touching me, so gently, makes me crave more of it. I don't want to fight in this moment. What I want is tenderness, gentleness, all the things I had as a little girl when my mother was still alive. The things I never got from my father.

I turn my cheek against his palm then press a kiss to the centre of it, watching as his gaze flares. He slides his hand into my hair, drawing me in for a kiss, soft and hot.

'I've never had this,' I whisper against his mouth. 'I've never had gentle or tender, not after Mama died.'

He eases my head back and looks down at me, his gaze searching my face. 'Then let me give you both, my wife. You can have all of it and more.'

He moves, turning me over onto my back. Then he rains kisses down on me, soft and sweet, my eyelids, my mouth, my neck, my throat. Going lower, kisses over my breasts and down over my stomach, before moving even lower. He kisses me gently, softly, his hands moving over me with light touches and caresses, giving me all the care and tenderness I could ever want.

I feel precious when he touches me like this. I feel cared for. I feel like a treasure, a work of art. I relax into his touch and the warmth of his body, the heat of his mouth and when at last, he moves inside me, I reach up and cup his face between my hands. Looking into his eyes as he builds the pleasure inside us both, I see my own passion reflected back at me. We are one in this moment and it feels like being finally whole. As if I've been missing another part of myself and never knew it until now.

He leans forward to kiss me, but I shake my head. 'No,' I murmur. 'I want to watch you come.'

His eyes gleam at that and so he holds my gaze, slowing his movements. But it's not desperate the way it was downstairs in his office. It's a journey we're going on together, building wonder as we go, lingering in each second of pleasure and enjoying the anticipation.

But like every journey, there's an end, I can feel it bearing down on me and I can see it bearing down on him too. But he's a master at this, I already know, and he times it just right, so at the ending of the road we meet and step over the edge together.

The world expands around us, bathing us in light, the silver in his eyes becoming incandescent as he falls with me, his arms gripping me tight.

CHAPTER SIXTEEN

Vincenzo

IT'S A BEAUTIFUL morning as I step out onto the terrace, the little gift I've bought for my beautiful wife safely in my pocket. It was delivered to me late last night and I can't wait to give it to her.

Maria has set a beautiful breakfast table for us with fresh brioche, coffee, jam and honey, fruit and all manner of other delicious breakfast things. There are mimosas also, so we have something to toast with, because I'll certainly be wanting to toast.

The past two days have been… Well, when I told her she was a revelation, I meant it. From the moment I took her dress off in my office, before laying her across my desk, she was flawless. Utterly beautiful. Then how sweetly she fell apart in my arms, saying my name, and the taste of her…

Fucking exquisite.

I *had* to give her my vow not to end her father's life just as she had to give me her vow to stay in my bed, because there simply wasn't another option. Not when her body was made for mine and vice versa. Besides, it's easy enough to make Salvatore disappear, and then I'll crush his allies.

Still, spending the rest of that day in bed with her was the happiest I can ever recall being. Even when she asked me about the scars on my back. I wasn't expecting her to say anything about them, but of course that was foolish of me. They're extremely visible and while I have no hang-ups about them, no one has ever asked me about them before. I didn't want to tell her, not when she was the indirect cause, but when my *gattina* asks me a question, I have to answer.

I didn't mean to make her cry, though, and I certainly didn't want her to either, not for me. It seems that beneath her fiery anger and her sharp claws, my wife has a soft heart, something I should have thought about when she demanded I spare her father. It broke me a little to see her pain, especially when she told me she'd had no tenderness, no gentleness, not since her mother died.

All I'd wanted to do in that moment was to give her everything she wanted. My family was the reason she'd missed out on all the things a mother should have given her, the reason her father had been so awful to her, and she needed some recompense for that.

So, I did give it to her. I worshipped her like the goddess she is, with as much care and tenderness as I was capable of, and I surprised even myself. At the end, when she looked into my eyes as we both came together…

You can never let her go now.

No. Never. I wasn't going to anyway, naturally, but

now I'm certain. She's a woman of great worth and she's mine, and I'll keep her at my side and in my bed. I'll give her everything she's ever wanted.

She thought you were a monster, though, remember? And you know she's not wrong...

But I don't want to think about that. Instead, I concentrate on my anticipation as I take the box out of my trouser pocket and place it in the middle of her plate. I left her sleeping this morning, so I could finish up making the necessary arrangements for her father's disappearance. Giovanni's new life will be an uncomfortable one, especially considering the identity I gave him has a record a mile long. They don't like drug dealers in Thailand, but I'm sure he'll agree that life in a Thai jail is better than death.

I go over to my chair and sit down, waiting for my wife to join me, but a couple of minutes pass and she doesn't arrive, so I get up again. I'm strangely restless, so I pace over to the edge of the terrace, to the stone parapet, and pause there a moment, glancing out to sea. Then I turn and pace back to the table, once more checking that everything is in place.

Then I hear a light footstep and when I look up, there she is in the doorway to the terrace. She's wearing a simple dressing gown of peacock-blue silk, with a silk belt loosely tying it closed. Her inky hair riots over her shoulders in the way I love so much, like thunderclouds I can actually touch and caress.

She blinks at me sleepily, then comes over to where I'm standing and lifts her arms, winding them around my neck as she rises on her toes to press a delicious kiss against my mouth. I take the kiss and deepen it, my hands resting on her hips as I tug her more firmly against me. She feels so good, all hot and silken and female, and I can already feel myself getting hard once again. My hunger for her is relentless. It feels as if I can never get enough.

After a few moments, I lift my head, looking down into her beautiful eyes. 'Breakfast first, *gattina.* You got a healthy workout last night.'

She flushes the colour of roses, the blue in her gown somehow turning her eyes a brilliant turquoise. 'I did. And I blame that solidly on you.'

'I didn't hear any protests.'

Her mouth curves in a smile that makes my chest ache. 'That's fair. There were none.'

I gently untangle her arms from around my neck, pausing to hold her fingers in mine and then turning her palms up and laying a kiss in the centre of each one. 'Sit, my wife. I'll pour you coffee.'

Still flushed, her eyes sparkling like rare gems, she goes to her chair and I insist on pulling it out for her. She sits, her gaze dropping to the little box in the middle of her plate.

'What's this?' she asks.

I round the table and sit down in my own chair, my anticipation building to ridiculous levels. 'A little gift,' I tell her. 'A wedding gift if you like.'

Her forehead creases. 'But I didn't get you anything.'

'Of course you didn't.' I lean forward, my elbows

on the table. 'You didn't know you'd be marrying me, remember?'

'True.' She glances down at the box again then picks it up and opens it. Her eyes widen and my pleasure and satisfaction pull tight.

Sitting in a cushion of black velvet are two rings. One a platinum wedding band studded with emeralds, the other a matching engagement ring with a huge emerald in the centre, surrounded by diamonds.

They're beautiful rings and they match her perfectly, making up for my error in getting a simple band when it should have been these all along. And naturally, I couldn't get just a wedding band. She needed an engagement ring too.

Caterina sits there, staring down at them, and I'm waiting for her face to flush with pleasure and her eyes to glitter with happiness. I'm waiting for her to take them out of the box and demand that I put them on her finger. I'm waiting for her to exclaim and hold out her hand, watching the sun catch the light in the jewels and making them sparkle.

But she does none of those things.

Instead she keeps looking at the rings and says nothing at all.

Something in my chest tightens, my muscles tensing. 'Well?' I ask, unable to keep the impatience from my voice. 'Do you like them?'

She doesn't look at me and disappointment kicks hard inside me. Then, hard on its heels, anger. I force them down, because maybe she's simply shocked, maybe that's all it is. Or maybe she doesn't like emeralds, or even rings. Maybe she doesn't wear jewellery at all and she's worried about my response.

'If you don't like the emeralds,' I offer, 'I can get you a different stone. Or maybe even earrings or a necklace if you don't wear rings. If you don't want jewellery at all then I can—'

'What does this mean, Vincenzo?' Finally, she lifts her gaze from her plate. There's no joy in her face, or even pleasure, no, it's anger that glitters in her eyes now.

My disappointment twists hard and part of me is shocked by its intensity. Shocked by how much I wanted her to like these, by how important her opinion has become to me. How important *she* has become and how quickly.

I don't like it. No one should be *that* important to me, no one. There's only one thing of any importance in my life and that's my crusade. Nothing comes before that.

So I shove the feelings aside and force a smile, leaning back in my chair as I clasp my hands together. 'It can mean anything you want it to mean.' My lazy tone has never felt so forced. 'I bought them because I thought you might like a prettier wedding band and an engagement ring to match.'

'Don't do that,' she says unexpectedly, her green gaze seeing right through me. 'Don't do that cynical amusement thing you do.'

A flash of anger hits me, even though I know she's right about the mask I wear, but I'm not happy with her pointing it out. 'I'm not doing anything, *gattina*. I'm merely disappointed that you don't like them.'

She stares at me then picks up her mimosa and takes a long swallow, toasting precisely nothing. 'It's not that I don't like them,' she says at last, putting her glass back down. 'They're beautiful.'

I know better than to let that mollify me. 'Then what's the issue?' I demand. 'If you don't want them, I can—'

'No. The issue is that I never agreed to marry you in the first place.'

'I know you didn't,' I say, my hold on my temper starting to fray. 'We've been through this. But the fact remains that we're husband and wife now.'

'So?' She's sitting rigid in her chair, her whole body looking as tense as mine feels. 'I never wanted that.'

'You were going to marry Bianchi,' I point out, a strange and totally out of proportion anger simmering in my gut. 'Which means you'd have ended up marrying anyway, so aren't you glad you ended up with me instead?'

'You're not listening. I never wanted to marry Carlo. I never wanted to marry *anyone*.'

'It's done now,' I say flatly. 'And it can't be undone.'

'Bullshit.' Her eyes glitter like the emeralds in the box, all sharp edges, anger flickering and leaping like a hot green fire. 'We can get a divorce and you can let me make my own choices.'

My whole body goes tight with negation. Divorce her? Let her go? The wolf in me growls with fury at the thought, but I try to reel it back in. This anger is pointless and why I'm letting it get to me is anyone's guess.

'No,' I say, putting every ounce of will I possess into the word. 'It's too late for that, Caterina.'

'Why?' she demands, her will matching mine strength for strength. 'I want to be free to make my own decisions, Vincenzo. I want a life that isn't…this.' She waves a hand at the villa surrounding us. 'I've already told you that.'

'You did, but my answer is the same. It's too late for you to have that life, not now you're married to me.' I hold her gaze so she understands how serious I am, because it's not just about me and what I want. Now she's married to me, it's an issue of personal safety. 'You're an Argenti and it doesn't matter if you divorce me. You'll always be an Argenti in the eyes of the families, and you'll always be a target. And I'm sorry, but I can't let you go only for someone to hurt you. I'll never agree to that.'

She takes a breath, continuing to stare furiously at me. 'Then give me a new name and a new life, the way you've done for others. That's easy for you to do and no one need ever know.'

For a minute I regret ever telling her about the people I've sent on to a new life elsewhere, because I could arrange that for her as I've arranged it for her father. But as I've told her, it's too late for that. It's too late for her to be free in the way she wants, because now she's mine.

Why is holding onto her so important?

I ignore the thought. 'And what will you do if in

three months' time you find yourself pregnant?' I demand instead, which is a low blow even if it's true. She could be pregnant. We didn't use any birth control, and I'll be damned if a child of mine is born outside the Argenti family.

She pales at that. 'If I'm pregnant, I'll let you know, of course. I'd never keep your child from you, Vincenzo.'

'But will you even keep it?' I'm being blunt and forceful, and these questions are difficult ones for her to answer, and I know that. But I don't care. If she's pregnant with my heir, I will take them both.

The rest of the colour leaves her face and she abruptly drops her gaze at the ring boxes again. 'I don't know,' she says more quietly. 'I haven't thought about it. I haven't thought about having children at all.'

'Which is not a risk I'm willing to take.' I don't disguise the iron in my voice. 'If you're pregnant, I'll keep the child and since a child should never grow up without their mother, I'll also keep you.'

She looks up at me again. 'And if I don't want to be kept?'

'You'll survive,' I tell her. 'Somehow, in this beautiful villa with a husband that keeps you well satisfied and where you won't have to worry about money, and you can have everything you've ever wanted.'

CHAPTER SEVENTEEN

Caterina

HE'S LOUNGING BACK in his chair with a casual arrogance that's both incredibly sexy and incredibly infuriating at the same time. Anger burns in his silver eyes, the hurricane force of his will howling against me from across the table.

But anger is burning a hole inside me too, along with a sliver of pain I can't identify. It's as if a splinter of glass has caught inside me, cutting me, putting holes in me, and it hurts.

The past two days have been so wonderful, nothing but lying in bed and making love, and talking with the Wolf about everything and nothing. He's a fascinating man, if opinionated, and we've had fun arguing with each other about little things that don't matter. And arguing is fun when you can make up afterwards in the most pleasurable way possible. But it was the tenderness he gave me that changed everything. I asked for it and he gave it to me, making me feel better than I have for years and years.

After I'd woken up this morning, I'd come downstairs to find him, wanting nothing more than to kiss him and lure him back to bed, only to walk onto a beautifully prepared terrace, with breakfast on the table, and a gift on my plate.

I didn't think anything of it initially, only a tight squeeze of pleasure that he'd bought something for me. Then I'd opened it and looked at what was inside and the happy little bubble I'd been inhabiting for the past two days abruptly popped.

I'm his *wife* and how could I have forgotten that? I'm married to a notorious man, whose only goal in life is to build empires and who'll let nothing stop him from doing that. And I can't ever leave, because no one leaves the *cosa nostra*, no one ever.

Being his wife means I'll never be free, and looking down at those rings, I could see that life stretching out before me, hemmed in by guards everywhere I go. I'll never be alone, never have a little flat with maybe a garden, never have a job or career of my own. I'll be relegated to being his trophy, kept safe and secure in that glass cabinet. Taken out to play with on occasion, but mainly being left there. And if we have children… Their lives would be forever at risk.

It's about more than that though, isn't it? None of this is about you.

I shove that thought away though, because why should I care? It doesn't matter what this is really about. I should have considered what he'd told me a couple of days earlier, about how I'd be his wife and rule the families at his side, or some such nonsense, and I'd let him distract me. I'd let myself be distracted by him.

But I can't do that any longer. I'm not staying here. I'm not going back to the life I had as a child, with all the expectations that were placed on me. All the boxes I was forced into or made to fit. I'm not going back to being punished for who I am either, not certainly not for him.

I stare into Vincenzo Argenti's eyes and hold his gaze with mine. 'Everything, except the one thing I actually want,' I say. 'My freedom.'

His anger flickers, the stark planes and angles of his face hardening. 'Freedom,' he echoes, saying the word like it's made of poison. 'What does it even mean? Who is ever free? There'll always be demands on you, always be other people you have to think about. Always things you have to do. No one is ever truly free, Caterina.'

'That's not what I'm talking about.' I'm frustrated now. 'I want to be free of the families. I want to have my own life, a normal life. One where I don't have to worry about being kidnapped or murdered, where I don't have to keep looking over my shoulder. Where I can make my own choices and decisions without someone else making them for me.'

His expression is like granite, the beautiful smile he gave me when I kissed him just before, vanishing as if it never was, and my heart aches at the change. This mask he wears as the head of his family, as the Wolf of Sicily, it's not him. It's not the tender, caring man who stroked me and kissed me as if I was made of glass, who argued with me passionately about something as ridiculous as whether chocolate was better than ice cream, who washed my hair in the shower last night, treating it like it was the most important task he'd ever done. It's not him and I don't like that. I want that other man back.

'That is not possible,' he says. 'And you know why it isn't. I've just told you why.'

My throat is tight but I don't want to cry, so I swallow it back. 'Of course it's possible,' I say sharply. 'You can give me a new identity. But you won't, will you? Because you can't bear to let what's yours go, isn't that right?'

He shifts in his chair as if I've said something uncomfortable, which is strange. He's possessive, all the men in the families are, and I know why. They value respect and honour, and the trophies they earn, not actual people.

'I can give you some freedom,' he says as if I've forced the words out of him. 'I can make sure any bodyguards give you space, and I'll—'

'No.' I don't care that I've interrupted him. 'That's not what I want and you know it. All my life I've been a thing, a pawn for my father, not a person, and I'm tired of it. I was told that if I wanted the deaths of Mama and Alessio to not be in vain, I had to do what he said. He made me responsible for fixing our entire family, and I'm tired of it, Vincenzo. I'm tired of having to do what everyone else wants me to do.'

'You're not a thing or a pawn, Caterina,' he says fiercely, leaning forward all of a sudden. 'And you don't have to fix anything here. You don't have to do anything but what you want here. That freedom I can certainly give you.'

My throat closes entirely, because I can see he wants to give that to me. But while it's something, it's not everything, and that's just not enough for me.

'That might be enough for a while,' I say. 'But what about in a year? Two years? What about in ten years?'

'What about it?' His gaze searches mine. 'What is scaring you so much, *gattina*? Is it only that this wasn't your choice? Or is there something more to it than that?'

I blink and take a breath. Having choices is very important to me since I've been deprived of them for so long, but I know he's right, that it's not only the lack of choices that bothers me. I have to face that thought now, the one I wanted to ignore, about how being his wife and being in his bed isn't really about *me*. Because what will happen as time goes on? When our physical hunger for each other fades? When we have children? When the march of his crusade goes on and on and on? What will our marriage end up being like then?

I take another shaky breath. 'I meant what I said, Vincenzo. Where will we be in five years? In ten? What about this crusade of yours? And if we have children, what about them?'

He frowns, not understanding me. 'The crusade will end eventually and I'll keep our children safe. I'll keep all of us safe, believe me.'

'I'm not talking about safety.' I don't want to have

this discussion, but I need to. *We* need to. My feelings are confused because all of this has happened so quickly. He's so much more than I ever imagined he'd be.

You're not falling for him already, are you?

No. No, definitely *not*. Again, he's not what I want in a man. There's too much death around him, too much violence, no matter how kind and caring he's been to me. I have to make him see reason about this marriage of ours, because I don't want to be tied to him forever.

'I'm talking about a relationship. About us being together.' I swallow, my mouth dry as I remember something else he told me. 'You said that love can never have any part in our relationship, and I… I don't want that. I don't want our children looking at us and seeing that we don't love each other.' My eyes prickle. 'I don't want a child of mine to ever look into their father's face and see only anger and resentment staring back.'

Shock crosses his face—he clearly didn't expect that—but just as quickly, his expression is wiped clean. 'Our children will survive,' he says in a hard, flat tone. 'Children can be remarkably resilient.'

'The same way you were resilient when your father laid his belt across your back?' I snap before I can think better of it.

Fury ignites in his gaze. 'I will *never* be like him.'

'No, but children being resilient sounds exactly like the kind of thing he'd say.' As soon as the words leave my mouth, I know I've gone too far.

Vincenzo shoves his chair back violently, the legs

scraping on the stone, then rises, his eyes gone molten with anger. He puts his hands on the table and leans in on them, the force of his will battering at me. 'I put a bullet between that man's eyes for what he did to my mother and I. Did you know that?'

I heave in a breath, shock flickering through me. Not that I hadn't heard the rumours about him, and he's alluded to it before. But it's different to hear the truth he's flinging at me now.

My mouth goes even drier. 'I've heard rumours. But what did he do to your mother?'

'He beat her down.' The Wolf's voice is sharp as a knife, his gaze stony. 'She loved him and he cut that love out of her heart and ground it into the dust. She was a beautiful, fiery, amazing woman and by the time she died, she was a broken shell. Because of him.'

I go cold. The only thing I knew about Stefano's wife as I grew up was that she'd died in a car bombing that my father had engineered. Yet it's clear from the look in Vincenzo's eyes that she was so much more than that. She was his mother and he loved her very much, and he loves her still.

'I'm sorry,' I say huskily, another little piece of my heart turning into glass and cutting me.

'Don't be sorry.' The bitterness in his voice is painful. 'It wasn't your fault, Caterina. Her death can be laid at Giovanni's door, it's true. But she died long before that. And that's no one's fault but my father's. That's why he had to die.' His mouth twists. 'Can you see the irony? I killed my father while you spared the life of yours.'

Oh, I can see it. Just as I see the shadows of grief and guilt and pain in his eyes. It cost him. It cost him to end his father's life and I suspect it costs him to end every life.

'Again, I'm sorry,' I say, my heart hurting for him though I'm not sure why. He shouldn't matter to me, not at all, yet somehow he's become more important to me than I ever thought possible. 'Not that he's dead. I'm sorry that there wasn't another way for you.'

Vincenzo's eyes widen slightly, as if he's not expecting the comment, then I see flashes of other emotions. But they're gone too fast for me to understand. 'Are you worried for my soul, *gattina*?' His voice has fallen back into that dark, cynical amusement again. 'If so, don't be. That's why I have a family priest, after all.'

He shoves himself upright, then rounds the table, pausing by my chair. I'm tense, my heart racing. I want to touch him, tell him it's okay, comfort him in some way. Anything to coax out the man behind that silver-eyed mask.

'Vincenzo,' I say softly. 'Please…'

He ignores me. Instead he reaches down and carefully, with a certain deliberateness, picks up the ring box with the beautiful rings in it. 'If you don't want these, that's fine. Annika might like them instead. She always was very fond of emeralds.'

Then he puts it in his pocket and strides back into the villa.

CHAPTER EIGHTEEN

Vincenzo

I LEAVE THE villa an hour later, heading over the lawn to the helicopter. I have business in Naples and I'm more than ready to forget what just happened between Caterina and I, lose myself in the day-to-day operation of my business.

The meetings I attend run all day and into the evening, ending only at midnight. But I'm too restless to fly back to the villa, not to mention too angry.

The volcanic fury sitting inside me is no one's responsibility but mine, and I need to get a handle on it somehow. After all, people tend to die when I get angry.

So, at three in the morning, I'm sitting in a rooftop bar, drinking vodka, watching the lights of the city spread out beneath me. The associates I was meeting with, and who've been drinking with me, have all left, mainly with women, and there's another woman beside me. She's almost in my lap and has making noises about going somewhere more 'comfortable', but I'm half-drunk and only half listening, because I can't stop thinking about Caterina.

The ring box is still in my pocket, my empty threat about giving the rings to Annika echoing in my ears. I was never going to give them to Annika. Those were bought for Caterina and Caterina alone. I only said that to her because I was furious and I wasn't sure why.

She told you you sounded like your father.

Fuck. That's true. I was already disappointed because she didn't want the rings or me, that she only wanted her so-called freedom, so that comment only kicked my rage into high gear. I'd built my life these last twenty years on *not* being him, never ever. So to tell me that I sounded just like him was… A red rag to a bull.

But that's not all she did.

I grit my teeth, not wanting to remember the look in her eyes after I told her that I'd shot Stefano. The look of pity that glowed there and her saying sorry that there hadn't been another way for me, as if she'd been concerned about me. About the effect killing my own father had on me.

She was right to be concerned. You're a monster.

My jaw aches and I down the glass of vodka in my hand. The liquid is ice-cold and it burns on the way down, but it does nothing to ease the leaden weight in my gut.

She's right to be concerned, but there's nothing I can do about it now. My hands are so red it doesn't matter whose blood is whose, and I accepted that as my role the day I picked up the gun and shot him with it.

What's done is done. There are no second chances, no shots at redemption, and there are none for her either.

Why not though? Why not give her the freedom she wants?

She's right, it would be simple, but I can't do it. I won't. She wouldn't be safe no matter how many new identities she has, and that's not even considering the fact that she might be pregnant.

The wolf growls a protective warning at the thought of children, and the man is in agreement. My child, out in the world and unprotected is a possibility I can't even think about. Just as I can't think of bringing up any child of mine without their mother, because I know just how painful that is.

So no, she's going nowhere. She's staying at my side and I will consider all the ways and means to give her as much freedom as I can, but that's as far as I'll go. And I'll make sure that what she said about her own father, about looking into his eyes and seeing only anger and resentment, will never happen to our child. I won't let it.

The woman next to me slides a hand up my thigh and leans in to whisper in my ear, promising me all kinds of naughty things. But both her hand and her voice leave me cold. I know the woman I really want and she's not here.

Perhaps I won't stay in Naples after all. Perhaps I'll fly back to the villa. There are many ways I can convince my wife that's she's better off with me. No one else can give her what I can. No one.

Gently but firmly, I take the woman's hand off my

thigh. I tell her she's beautiful, but I'm married and I will not be taking her to bed. She pouts a little, then leaves to find another, more receptive man.

I exit the bar, slightly amazed at myself for refusing what she was offering on the grounds that I'm married. Which I am, of course, but I never anticipated that I'd actually be faithful to the wife I kidnapped. And I am.

I don't want another woman, I realise. I don't want anyone else but the woman I married. My Caterina. Now, at the thought of her and the pleasure we shared, my body is waking despite how tired and half-drunk I am. It never woke for that other woman. Not even a flicker.

I organise the helicopter and soon I'm flying through the dark night back to Sicily.

I land just as dawn is breaking. I debate the merits of taking some time to sleep before seeing her, but I can't wait, so I proceed up the stairs to my bedroom—our bedroom—to wake her. But she isn't there.

Discomforted and unreasonably annoyed by her absence, I cross the hallway to her room and push open the door. But she's not there either.

A flicker of alarm goes through me. Where is she? Has she managed to escape somehow? But that's impossible. My security is second-to-none and they would have informed me if she'd somehow left.

I go downstairs and ask one of my guards where my wife is, only to have him inform me that she woke early and wanted to go for a walk on the beach at the base of the cliffs. No, she is not alone. Yes, she has eyes on her.

The relief that sweeps through me is impossible to deny, yet I have no time to think about why that is. Instead, I go quickly to the stone path that zigzags down the steep cliffs to the beach.

It's where I used to walk with my mother, barefoot in the silky golden sand with the waves crashing on the shore. Back before I become the wolf and she became a husk of a woman. Before my father beat the both of us into the shapes he wanted us to be. Me, his perfect heir. Her, his perfect wife.

There are guards at the base of the path and I nod my approval as I go past them. I can see her now, dressed in some kind of billowy, white nightgown that the wind catches, walking slowly along the sand, her back to me. She has her arms wrapped around herself, though the wind isn't cold, and I watch as she pauses and turns to face the sea.

She looks so like my mother, the way she's standing and gazing out at the ocean like a desert island survivor looks for rescue. It sends a spear of ice right through me.

You know what you're doing to her, don't you?

I stop dead in the sand as the realisation comes to me. An unwelcome realisation. Because of course I know what I'm doing to her.

If she's standing here on the beach, looking for rescue just like my mother, then I am my father, keeping her here. I am my father, accepting the parts of her that I like and rejecting the rest. Her need for freedom, her need to have a normal life, her need to feel safe.

I want her passion, her fire and her anger, yet I also

want her to obey me, to stay here at my side, to accept the fact that I'm the head of the family and I decide what happens, not her.

The spear of ice twists inside me and a burst of pain radiates out through my chest, squeezing my heart.

It happened gradually to my mother. Stefano slowly crushed the life out of her with his insistence that she never argue with him. He was the head of the family and as his wife she had to obey, and even though he never hit her, his constant belittlements and criticisms took their toll.

Her failure to give him more children incensed him and so he exiled her here to the villa, making her stay so the doctors could examine her and give her special diets, and on occasion sedate her to keep her 'calm'. All so she could conceive.

He didn't stay with her. He kept her like a princess in a tower, his brood mare that he would visit every week to encourage a conception.

She loathed being a prisoner. That's why she and I would walk along the beach every day. As a child I'd thought nothing of it since she'd make each walk an adventure, but in retrospect I knew that she paced the beach like a tiger pacing around the bars of a cage.

Until my father decided that she should join him in Rome for some big family meeting and the car she was in exploded. I was devastated when I learned she'd died. But now, with the benefit of hindsight, I wonder if in that moment of death she felt finally free.

You cannot do that to Caterina.

The world slows and stops as I stare at the tall,

slender figure of my wife, standing and looking out to sea. The wind blows her black hair around her face and makes her nightgown billow around her calves, and the spear of ice in my chest begins to melt, filling my veins with ice water.

I try to ignore it, pushing the thoughts away as I make myself continue on to where she stands. She must have seen my approach but she doesn't turn, her attention still on the distant horizon.

Dawn is flaming, the sun rising from the sea, red and pink shading the dense dark blue of the sky. Another beautiful sunrise, but all she is looking at are the bars of her cage, isn't she?

'My mother and I used to walk along this beach,' I say after a moment. 'We would look for shells and sea glass and pretty stones. Sometimes I'd pretend to be a pirate, and I'd kidnap her in my pirate ship, but then we'd become friends. She'd draw maps in the sand and tell me about all the places we'd sail to, and have adventures there.'

The waves lap against the sand. The tide is coming in. If she's not careful, my wife will get her feet wet, yet she doesn't seem to notice.

'That sounds idyllic,' she says, still looking out over the sea.

'It was.' I pause a moment. 'Until I realised that my mother was trapped here and she came to the beach to feel free.'

Slowly, Caterina turns to me, her hair blowing around her face. Her green eyes are shadowed, and there are dark circles under them. 'Why was your mother trapped here?'

I push my hands into my pockets. 'My father wanted more children and decided that she needed to stay here being looked after by doctors and having her diet monitored. She'd be sedated sometimes too. He thought that would make it more likely for her to conceive. He used to visit her once a week.'

'That's awful.'

'Yes.' I meet her gaze. 'She couldn't leave and nothing she did or said could make my father change his mind. She had three miscarriages and after that, fell into a deep depression. After five years of being trapped here, my father eventually brought her to a family meeting in Rome and that's when she was killed by the car bomb.'

There are flickers of pity and horror in Caterina's eyes, and no wonder. Not considering her own position here and the similarities between my mother and herself.

'Is that how you're going to treat me?' she asks bluntly.

I'm expecting the question, so I don't hesitate. 'No. Of course not. I would never do that to you.'

'And yet that's what you're doing. I'm trapped here. You won't even consider giving me my freedom.'

You know she's right.

I know she is, I know. Yet I can't accept her leaving me. 'You're not trapped here, *gattina*,' I remind her and myself. 'You can leave. With the appropriate security, naturally. You're not a prisoner.'

She turns fully to face me now, her arms still wrapped around herself. I can see goose bumps rising on her skin, so I slip my jacket off and move over to her, putting it around her shoulders.

She doesn't resist, looking up at me. 'I'm just an object to you, aren't I? Just a thing. A wife at your side, a sex toy in your bed and an incubator for your children.'

She's so direct, so blunt, but she's wrong.

'No,' I say, suddenly fierce. 'That's not how I think of you.' Her jaw is tight, her body stiff with anger, but I reach for her, pulling her against me. She's so warm and despite my tiredness, my cock is hard and getting harder. I grip her hips firmly, feeling the softness and heat of her skin beneath her thin nightgown. The fabric is slightly transparent and I can see the pink of her nipples through it, and I feel suddenly feral at the thought of all my guards being able to see them too.

'What you want matters,' I say to her, meaning every word. 'I can work it so that our life will be as normal as possible, I promise. You'll never be a prisoner here. If you like, I can find you an apartment anywhere in the world that can be yours and yours alone. And you can visit it anytime you want.'

Her body is still stiff with resistance, her features set, so I lift my hands from her hips and cup her face between my palms. Emotions move through her green eyes, fury, pain, sadness. They are precious, these emotions of hers, and I want to ease her. Soothe her in any way I can, which is unlike me.

'I can make it easy for you,' I murmur, bending to her mouth and pressing a soft kiss there. 'I can make it so you'll be freer than you've ever felt in your life.' Another kiss. 'There are no bars on this cage, *gattina.*' Another kiss to her jaw. 'There is no cage at all.'

CHAPTER NINETEEN

Caterina

HIS HANDS CUPPING my face are warm and his mouth making its way down the side of my neck is hot. The kisses he presses against my skin burn and my body is starving for him.

After he walked away from our breakfast yesterday morning, I heard the helicopter come and go, and realised he had left the villa. I checked with Maria and indeed, he'd apparently gone to Naples for the day on business. And no, she didn't know when he was coming back.

My disappointment that he'd gone seemed out of all proportion, so I tried to tell myself that I was glad. He'd left in a huff after I hadn't liked his rings, and he'd taken them with him, and if he gave them to his stupid mistress, who cared? Certainly I didn't.

But as the day progressed and I couldn't seem to settle, wandering around the villa restlessly with a pressure in my chest that was starting to turn into pain, I was forced to admit to myself that actually *I* cared.

I cared that I'd upset him. I cared that his father had been such a terrible person, that he'd lost his mother, that he was clearly still grieving her. I cared that he'd been turned into a killer because of an accident of birth, and I was starting to suspect that it wasn't in his nature.

I went in search of Maria in the end, and had a conversation with her about Vincenzo as a boy, since she'd been their housekeeper since he'd been a child. He'd been a kind little boy, she'd told me. He'd rescued a kitten once, and loved his mother. He'd had a puppy for a while until his father took it away to train it into a 'proper' dog, and it came back and killed one of the cats he'd rescued. He'd been inconsolable.

The only time his mother had been happy, Maria told me, was when she was with him, and he was the only one who could make her laugh.

It hurt to hear those stories. It hurt to hear what his father had taken from him and his mother, and it made me so angry too. It was lucky that Stefano Argenti was already dead, because if I'd had a weapon, I'd certainly have taken it, found him and shot him myself.

After that I'd put on a swimming costume and gone down to the pool, swimming laps and then floating on my back the way I remembered from long ago. I kept waiting for his voice to follow me, to see him coming down the steps from the villa, but there were only his guards, keeping watch.

I was disappointed. I was so bitterly disappointed and I didn't know why.

Eventually, after realising he wasn't coming back here anytime soon, I let Maria cook me dinner and I watched TV until late, trying to distract myself. Then I'd gone to bed. I didn't use his bedroom, but the one I'd been given.

My dreams were full of darkness and I was running down a shadowed hallway, trying to escape from something or someone. And then the dream changed so that I was the one doing the chasing. I'd woken just before dawn, feeling unrested and groggy, so I'd gone down the stone path to visit the beach, needing some fresh air to clear my head. It was such a beautiful beach that I'd stayed to watch the sunrise, trying to ignore the guards that stood on the stone path, looking down at my every move.

And just when I was thinking about going back up to the villa, out of the corner of my eye I could see a man walking towards me. Tall and powerful, moving with that familiar lithe grace.

My heart had jumped in my chest and when he came to stand beside me, I'd been filled with the inexplicable urge to turn and throw myself into his arms. But I'd forced the urge away. I didn't want him to think anything had changed from when he'd walked away the day before.

Then he'd told me about his mother and how they'd used to go walking on this beach, and in my head I could see him, a little boy running beside her as they found treasures in the sand. Then watching in delight as she drew him maps and told him of all the places they would visit.

A little boy's dream. But only a dream, because his mother had been held prisoner here and all because of his father.

My chest had tightened and it's still tight now as he presses another kiss at the base of my throat. His body is so hard and hot, a delicious contrast to the cold wind blowing around me. I can smell the smoke and cedar of his scent surrounding me, in the jacket he placed around my shoulders and on his skin, and all I want is to melt into his arms. All I want is to believe the promises he's murmuring, because right now the thought of leaving him is not one I want to contemplate.

But then I smell another scent, a feminine one, and a surprisingly sharp knife of jealousy slides between my ribs. 'So,' I whisper as he presses another kiss to my throat. 'You really meant it when you said you were going to give the emeralds to your mistress.'

He goes still for a moment and lifts his head. 'Is that jealousy I hear, *gattina?*' He's amused, but I am most definitely not, though I wish I could be.

'I know I said you weren't to sleep with anyone else on our wedding night, but even two days later it's—'

He lays a finger across my mouth, silencing me. 'I was approached, little wolf. And while I didn't encourage her, I didn't exactly push her away either. At least, not until she made her intentions known and then I decided to come home.' His gaze turns intense. 'To you.'

The jealousy eases, but I'm angry that I even felt it. I'm angry that it even matters to me, but I'm starting to realise there's a reason for that.

A reason my heart leapt when he came across the sand to me.

A reason I was disappointed he'd left yesterday.

A reason all I wanted was to throw myself into his arms today.

You are *falling for him. You idiot.*

I want to deny it. I want to deny it with all my heart, but I know the truth deep inside me. He's made me love him with his acceptance of me as I am, with his unexpected gentleness and tenderness, with his ability to join me in ridiculous arguments, and with his wicked hands and his beautiful mouth.

He's made me love him and I don't know what I can do to escape it. In fact, I have a horrible feeling I can't do anything about it at all.

His black brows draw together, and I know a moment's intense fear that he's guessed what I'm feeling right now. And he can't know, he just can't, because he promised me love wouldn't be a part of our marriage, and I don't know what he'll do if he finds out. For once, I don't want to push.

So I open my mouth and nip at the fingers across my lips and I watch his gaze flare with desire. 'I've had no sleep in the last twelve hours and I'm probably still half-drunk,' he says. 'But all I can think about is you naked in my bed, so you'd better take me back up to the villa or else you'll find yourself flat on your back in the sand.'

'That sounds uncomfortable,' I murmur.

He smiles and takes my hand. 'Maybe later we'll test the theory, but not now.'

Then he leads me back up to the villa.

In the privacy of his bedroom, he pulls me into the shower, washing the sand from my feet, while I squeeze shower gel in my hands and run it all over his body. Stroking the hard planes of his chest and stomach, then his muscled arms before turning him around and washing his powerful back. The scars from his father's belt are deep and I touch them lightly, caressing them, and he doesn't stop me. And he doesn't resist when I put my mouth to them, kissing them, because even though they're marks of pain and punishment, they are part of him and so I think I love them too.

I turn him around again, so he's facing me, his silver eyes blazing.

'I like it when you stay where I put you,' I say, teasing him.

He smiles, that one I particularly like, sexy and hot and just for me. 'And I like it when you do what I say. Get down on your knees for me, my wife. It's time for you to service your husband.'

A thrill of pleasure goes through me and I drop to my knees, because I have no trouble at all obeying his every sensual command. No, I like it. It turns me on and since my pleasure is his, he delights in it.

I take his hard cock in my hand and guide it to my mouth and draw him in, loving the way his features tense as I wrap my lips around him. His skin is smooth and velvety in my mouth, tasting of crisp salt and his own special masculine flavour.

I use my tongue and my teeth to tease him, watching him as I do, and when he slides his hands into my hair to guide me, I lean in. I grip his powerful thighs, taking him deeper, loving the way he growls in response. Then I lick and suck him, working him over, until he suddenly pulls away. His hands are hauling me up from my knees, before turning me and pushing me hard against the tiled wall of the shower. Then he lifts me straight up so I can wind my legs around his waist, and he pins me to the wall, his thick, hard cock pushing deep inside me.

I gasp in pleasure, clenching around him, loving the feeling of him inside me. His eyes are dark silver now and inches from mine, and all I can see is pleasure in them. The pleasure *I* give him.

'Let's see,' he whispers fiercely. 'Let's see if we can't create the most beautiful child right here, right now.'

And I'm so lost in the pleasure, lost in him, that all I can do is lean forward and kiss him hungrily, my thighs holding him to me as he thrusts in, deep and hard. His mouth on mine is urgent, like that first time in the pool, and I'm meeting him hunger for hunger. There's a beautiful madness in the way he fucks me, the pleasure building and building, making my nails claw at his back, catching on those terrible scars, yet he doesn't flinch.

'Harder,' he growls against my mouth. 'Scratch me, little wolf. Mark me. Give me your pain, not his.'

And I want to take that pain away from him, give him something else in return, something better, so I do. Then the orgasm comes, smashing us both into oblivion as I clutch him and whisper his name.

CHAPTER TWENTY

Vincenzo

I WAKE SOMETIME in the late afternoon, the sun shining through a crack in the linen curtains of my bedroom, turning the white sheets golden.

My Caterina lies beside me, still asleep, the black storm of her hair lying over my white pillows. The sheet has fallen off her, exposing her naked body as she lies on her side facing me. Her skin looks as if it has been gilded by a master painter, highlighting all her delicious curves, her breasts, her hips, her thighs, the delicate line of her cheek.

She is so beautiful.

I'm filled with a pleasant post-orgasmic haze, unable to stop thinking about her nails scratching my back in the shower, criss-crossing the scars I already have with the scars she gave me. I want those scars of hers. I want the pain of her nails on my skin, cancelling out the pain of my father's belt. And I want the child we hopefully created between us, new life after all these years of death.

But what if she's not pregnant? Will you keep her here like your father kept your mother?

The pleasant haze fragments as a cold thread of unease winds through me.

I wouldn't do that, of course I wouldn't. If she's not pregnant then it's fine, we can try again and I'm all for trying as many times as it will take since isn't that the best part?

I throw back the sheet and get out of bed, stalking into the bathroom. I splash some water on my face to get rid of the lingering effects of sleep, but I can't stop thinking about her, standing on the beach, looking out to sea. Her telling me that a facsimile of freedom isn't what she truly wants, no matter what I can promise her.

You know what she truly needs. That's to be free of you.

I brace my hands on the black marble vanity and look down unseeing into the basin. What she wants is impossible. She's forever tied to me as my wife now, and if she's pregnant—

You forced her into marriage, screwed her without a condom, told her that freedom for her is impossible, and that she'll never be loved. All of this is about what you *want. None of this is about her.*

I'm cold inside and getting colder, and I could lie to myself, deny that I feel anything at all for her and that there's no escaping the situation, no escape for her, but…

I'm not sure I can lie anymore or pretend she's not important to me. Act as if her feelings mean nothing, when they in fact mean everything.

She means everything.

I slowly lift my head and stare in the mirror at the man looking back. The face of the monster I've become. The Wolf of Sicily.

I have my father's eyes, his colouring and his height. I have nothing at all of my mother, except perhaps my heart, which was once as fierce and tender as hers. But it's not anymore. There's only a stone where my heart should be, hard and cold and impervious. Like my father's heart.

You know what you have to do.

Everything inside me goes tight, my chest aching as if a bullet has torn a hole right through it, but there's no escaping the truth and I know it.

I want to keep her here. I want to keep here with me forever, but if I do that, I'll be my father through and through. She won't ever taste that freedom she so badly wants. She won't ever have that little flat or a career, or a life outside the *cosa nostra.* All she'll ever have is a husband who keeps her at his side and gives her nothing in return.

I know what she needs, even though she might not know it herself. The thing that's been missing in her life since my family destroyed hers. She needs love, and that's the one thing I can't give her. Because slowly but surely the Argentis kill love. They strangle it, starve it and beat it to death. Then, once it's dead, we fill the space it left with violence and murder, with sorrow and pain.

That's the true Argenti legacy. *My* legacy.

And I can't involve Caterina or any children we

may have in that legacy. I can't pass that on to the next generation. I promised myself the violence would end with me, but I know that if I keep her, it won't. It will go on and on, down through our children and there will never be an end to it. The shadow Stefano Argenti casts is too long and I can't escape it.

It has to stop. Now. Here. With her.

Ice fills my veins, my cold stone of a heart pumping it around the rest of my body, and I let it. I'm not the wolf now, I'm the man, and the man has a purpose to fulfil. He cannot let himself be distracted from it and he cannot let anyone get in his way.

I push myself away from the vanity and go back into the bedroom. Caterina is stirring, giving a sensual little stretch as she does so. Then she sees me standing next to the bed and smiles, reaching out for me. 'Come back to bed,' she says. 'I need my husband.'

But her husband is gone. I can't be him any longer, no matter how badly she wants him.

She must see something in my expression, because her black brows draw together in a frown, her green eyes full of concern. She sits up, drawing the sheet about her. 'Vincenzo? What's wrong? Has something happened?'

Hearing her say my name makes my resolve falter, but only for a second. There can be no second-guessing and no regrets, not now. This is the right thing to do, the *only* thing to do.

'Sadly, I've had a small change of heart,' I drawl. 'You wanted your freedom, so I've decided you shall have it. I'll organise a new identity for you, a new passport and a new life. You can have the normality you wanted.'

She blinks, shock slowly filling her gaze. 'What?' The word sounds blank, as if she doesn't understand what I've said.

'A new identity,' I explain patiently, my voice cold. 'That's what I gave your father and that's what I'll give you. You're right. You should have the normal life you wanted and I'm going to give it to you.'

She blinks again, understanding dawning across her face. 'But…you said that was impossible. You said that if I was pregnant—'

'I know what I said.' My voice sharpens, a hot flare of temper penetrating the ice I've surrounded myself with. 'But I was wrong. I don't want to do to you what my father did to my mother. I don't want to imprison you here.'

'I won't be a prisoner,' she says, as if it's self-evident. 'You said yourself you'll give me as much freedom as you're able to manage.'

'But you didn't want that, remember?' The cold in me is beginning to melt no matter how hard I try to hold onto it, fury coming hard on its heels, thick and hot. 'You've made no secret of the fact that it's not enough for you.'

Colour is leaching from her face, making her green eyes seem even greener. 'Yes, I did say that, but… Maybe I've changed my mind.'

My fury leaps higher. I was expecting her to grab her freedom with both hands, not suddenly decide she doesn't want it after all. Which is unacceptable.

The wolf is elemental, savage with sharp teeth and claws, and it doesn't understand what I'm doing. It doesn't understand why I'm sending her away, when all it wants is to keep her.

But I'm not the wolf now and I refuse to be Stefano, and so there's only one way this is going to go.

'That's too bad,' I say coldly. 'I've made my decision.'

She's sitting rigidly upright, the sheet now clutched in her hands. 'I like the villa and I like you. I like being your wife.' Her tone is light, but there's a strange current running through the words.

'Since when did you suddenly like being here with me?' I shouldn't keep arguing with her, not when nothing she says will change my mind, but I can't seem to stop. 'When not a few hours ago you were telling me that it wasn't enough?'

Her mouth tightens and she looks down at her hands clutching the sheet. 'You're right. If I'm pregnant then—'

'Caterina,' I say roughly, unable to let go of the sense that she's hiding something from me. 'Givc me the truth.'

She continues to stare down at the sheet for a long moment. Then abruptly, as if she's come to some decision, she lifts her head and meets my gaze. There's some powerful emotion burning in her green eyes. It's fierce, hot, determined, and it momentarily steals my breath clean away.

She lifts her chin. 'The truth? Okay, here's the truth.

I changed my mind because I think I'm in love with you, Vincenzo. And now I don't want to leave you.'

The shock of it guts me. All I can do is stand there staring at her, the words echoing in my head. That thought that she might fall for me, the man who did all those terrible things to her and her family, never occurred to me, not once. And for a second I can't believe it, that she must be lying to me in some way, but there's nothing but truth in those beautiful eyes of hers.

It's too late. You've hurt her. Irrevocably.

There's an agony somewhere inside me, but I ignore it. I have to. The Argenti legacy must be more than all the violence and death my father perpetuated and it must be more than what I've perpetuated myself. And it has to start right here, right now, no matter how much she loves me.

I give her a slight but regretful smile. 'Unfortunate,' I say. 'But nothing that can't be fixed. You'll have to forget me, *gattina,* since I will not be featuring anywhere in this new life of yours.'

Her gaze is very fixed and she sits still as a statue. Then abruptly, she drops the sheet, leaps from the bed, coming over to stand in front of me. She's beautifully naked, her hair tumbling around her shoulders and falling in an inky waterfall down to her waist. Her eyes blaze with the spirit of the warrior inside her; she's ready to fight a battle and she's ready to fight hard.

'No,' she says fiercely. 'I won't go. I want to stay here with you.'

But it's a battle she can't win, because I am a warrior too, and I'm stronger. I have the scars to prove it.

'I don't care,' I say coldly, clearly. 'If you won't go then I'll make you.'

The blaze in her eyes falters as she looks at me, finding no give in my expression. 'Vincenzo…' She lifts a hand to my face. 'Please…'

I stand rigid as her fingers brush my skin and there's a part of me that wants nothing more than to kiss her palm, pull her close, tell her I've changed my mind after all.

But I can't. This is the way it has to be and after all, I'm used to pain.

'I'm going to organise some documents for you,' I say, my voice flat with control. 'Pack your things.'

Then I turn and stride out of the bedroom.

CHAPTER TWENTY-ONE

Caterina

I STARE AT the doorway as he retreats through it, shock still reverberating through me. My heart feels as if he took it between his strong hands and ripped it in two, and I can't stop trembling.

Stumbling back, I sit on the bed, my eyes prickling.

I knew when he came out of the bathroom and I saw that frighteningly cold expression on his face that he'd decided something. But I never thought his decision would be giving me my freedom. And I never thought that the moment he said it, I wouldn't want it.

Part of me is angry with myself for telling him I loved him, that I should have protected myself, kept myself safe. But another part of me, the braver part, the part of me that discovered true freedom in his arms, doesn't regret a thing.

He was never going to change his mind for me, no matter what I told him, and so the outcome would have been the same either way. At least now he knows that he's not alone, that he's got someone, somewhere, out in the world, who loves him more than she ever thought it was possible to love someone.

I close my eyes, tears forming behind my lids and falling, no matter how I try to stop them. I shouldn't be crying. He's giving me exactly what I always told him I wanted, and really, I should be rejoicing. Yet… I just wish getting what I wanted didn't come at the expense of my heart.

For long minutes I sit there as my tears fall, debating the merits of going after him and arguing with him, try to figure out a way to change his mind, but what's the point?

I'm not going to force myself on another man who doesn't want me, not after how my father treated me. And I'm tired of fighting for the things *I* want too. He gave me a taste of what being cared about feels like, so I can take that with me when I go, and anyway, perhaps he's right. Perhaps with time it'll fade. Perhaps a new life, a normal life, will make up for his loss.

You know nothing will make up for it.

But I can't afford to accept that right now, because if I do, I'll lose all hope and without hope, I'm nothing.

I weep for a bit on the edge of the bed, then I pull myself together. I go back to my bedroom and have a shower, and try to think about packing some things. But the only thing I want from here is him, so in the end I pack nothing at all.

Sometime later a meal is delivered to my room, but I don't touch it.

Part of me is hoping he'll come upstairs and knock on my door, tell me he's changed his mind, but even though I wait up till midnight, no knock comes. And eventually I fall asleep, dreaming of his hands touching me, his mouth on my skin.

The next morning a security guard finds me, telling me that my documents are ready and I'll be flying to Rome, and from there, to the US, where my new life will begin.

In my little sheaf of documents is a note on a business card. The note says: *if you are pregnant, call this number.* There's no name on the card, nothing else but the number, written in bold slashes like the note he slipped under my door only a few nights ago. It feels like a lifetime now.

So that's it. That's all I'm left with. A note and a new life, the freedom I always wanted, and yet…

Something in me rebels, something that isn't done fighting, because what will that freedom mean if he's not there? What will my new life look like if he's not in it? I'll have that career and a flat, and maybe flatmates. I'll even have a cat and one day a boyfriend, but…

I don't want it. I don't want it with everything in me. I know what I want now, what I *really* want, and it's him. His magic touch and his silver eyes. The challenges he throws me, the arguments he gives me. The tenderness and the kindness he doesn't even realise he's capable of.

Walking away would be so easy. I could take this new life he's presented me with and not argue. I could give up. Surrender. Go wherever he's decided to put me without a fight, but…

I've done nothing but fight him since I got here, so

am I really going to give up now? Let him chase me away? Sure, I don't want to force myself on someone who doesn't want me, but he *does* want me. And more than that, he needs me, I know he does. He's got no one else, no one at all, no one who knows his true heart the way I know it. The way I've discovered it over these past few days.

He's never had someone fight for him. He's never had someone stay because they want to be with him, because he's more important than anything, and he *is* more important. *Love* is more important and I love him.

He is my freedom and I'm not leaving.

Slowly and with care, I rip the note up into little pieces, toss them onto the floor and then I leave the room to find him.

He's going to give me the fight of my life, but this time I'm going to win.

I'll make sure of it.

CHAPTER TWENTY-TWO

Vincenzo

I SIT AT my desk, sipping my morning coffee, every part of me concentrated on the sound of the helicopter outside on the lawn. It should be leaving any moment now, taking my Caterina away to her new life.

It was the right thing to do, the *only* thing to do. She wasn't meant to be here with me, her beautiful spirit slowly fading the way my mother's did, trapped in a life she didn't want, with a husband she never asked for.

My chest aches, a nagging dull pain that doesn't go away no matter how many times I rub it. And I can't get away from how she looked yesterday, standing in front of me so naked and beautiful, telling me she wanted to stay. Telling me that she loved me. Then the brush of her fingers against my cheek…

The pain in my chest intensifies. I drain my coffee then shove my chair back, because the helicopter is still there, it hasn't left yet and it should be on its way. I need it to leave so I can get her out of my head, and get back to the business of planning my crusade.

I go to the door and fling it open, mentally preparing myself to find out what the delay is, only to find Caterina on the other side.

She's still wearing her nightgown and her hair falls over her shoulders in a black waterfall. She blazes like a torch. Her green eyes meet mine and before I can open my mouth, she slaps her palms on my chest and shoves me back into my office. Then she steps through the doorway and slams the door after her.

I draw myself up to my full height, every muscle rigid. 'What the hell are you doing?' I demand. 'You're supposed to be leaving—'

'No,' she interrupts. 'I'm not going anywhere.' She's standing with her shoulders square, her hands now in fists at her side, and when she speaks, her voice is fierce. 'And if you think you can get rid of me that easily, you've got another think coming.'

The pain in my chest gets worse, my fury rising. 'You're leaving,' I say, trying to keep a hold of my temper. 'Get on that fucking helicopter. Do as I say!'

Her chin lifts, green eyes full of fire, a warrior about to do battle. 'Make me.'

And I want to put my hands on her hips, toss her over my shoulder, carry her to the helicopter and put her in it, except I know the moment I touch her, I won't be able to. I'll want to grip her and draw her close and keep her. Keep her forever.

'You can't, can you?' She stares furiously up at me. 'Because you don't want me to go.'

It's not a question and my jaw tightens. 'Odd. That

must be why I arranged all those documents for a new life for you in—'

'Vincenzo,' she says and before I can move away, she's lifted a hand to my cheek the way she did yesterday, her fingers brushing my skin. 'I'm not leaving you.'

Something twists hard in my chest, an agony blazing as bright as her eyes.

'You have to,' I force out through gritted teeth. 'I won't keep you trapped here with me. I won't keep you in this life you never wanted.'

'But what if I do want it?' Her palm is warm against my cheek. 'What if I want you?'

My hands close into fists as I try to keep them from reaching for her. 'You can't,' I say forcefully. 'I killed my own father. I shot him, Caterina. And there are many other things I've done, so many things—'

'I don't care.' She stares right into my eyes, seeing into the heart of me. 'You're trying to change things, trying to make things better.'

'If I keep you here,' I grit out, 'I'll be just like him.'

'You were never like him, Vincenzo.' She's suddenly fierce. 'Never. You saved me and you tried to save my mother and brother. You showed me how strong I really was, and you made me feel wanted for the first time in my life.' There are tears in her eyes now, even though her gaze still burns. 'And that freedom I wanted? I found it with you.'

I can see the emotion that lights up her face, pure and bright, making her even more lovely than she already is. *Dio*, she's always fought for what she wanted

And now she's fighting for you.

'You shouldn't,' I hear myself say, my voice full of gravel. 'You deserve better than me. You deserve more than—'

'You don't get to tell me what I do and don't deserve,' she interrupts yet again, her thumb stroking across my cheek. 'I decide that and I've decided that what I deserve is to be your wife.'

I shouldn't be doing this. I shouldn't be letting her touch me like this. I shouldn't be letting her say all these things, each word eroding my resolution bit by bit. Eroding my certainty that what I'm doing is right. Eroding my resistance to her.

I thought I was strong enough to let her go, but I don't think I am after all. 'It won't be the life you want,' I say, trying to make her see reason. 'I don't know how long it will take to bring the families under my control, and they're not going to go quietly. There'll never be peace, which means there'll never be peace for you.'

She steps even closer, the warmth of her body and her scent surrounding me. 'Don't give me excuses, Vincenzo,' she murmurs. 'You don't have to be afraid.'

I want to tell her that I'm not afraid, that I'm not afraid of anything, but deep inside, I know that's not true.

I am afraid. I'm afraid I'm not worthy of her.

The scent of her is making me dizzy, making me want to reach out and pull her close, crush her mouth under mine. 'I can't love you,' I force out, knowing even as I say it that it's an excuse. 'I told you. Love is the one thing I can't give you.'

'It's okay,' she says as if it's nothing at all. 'I have enough love for both of us.'

I stare down into her face and a certain exhaustion winds through me as I think about what it would be like if I made her get on that helicopter. If I made her leave. There would be no more fights, no more challenges. No bright, fiery woman to come home to or to argue with. No touches or kisses, or her warmth in my arms. No seeing that emotion, that love in her eyes.

She needs more from you than that.

I take a breath, but I can't seem to get air, as the wolf fights and claws its way out of the cage I've put it in. It wants her, it always has, and more… It loves her and the man…

Loves her too.

'Caterina…' My voice is hoarse and I don't know what I'm trying to say. It feels as if a bucket of ice water has been emptied over my head and I struggle to breathe through the shock. And I know it's true, it's always been true.

I fell in love with her the moment I saw her in the pool, floating on her back, like a mermaid. Or maybe even before that, when I married her, and I realised the worth of the woman I'd just kidnapped.

I thought Stefano had killed all love and light in my life, and yet it's here in my stone of a heart, a new tendril curling hopefully towards the sun. And as I accept that it's there, it comes to me.

It was never sending her away that made me not like my father.

It was loving her. Because he didn't know the meaning of the word.

But Caterina taught me what it meant and what it felt like. Love was her kissing the scars on my back and that look in her eyes and everything she is. Love is the warrior spirit within her, the perfect match for the wolf in me.

Love is the way she's looking at me right now and refusing to leave me, challenging me the way she's always done right from the first.

And me… I can never resist her challenge.

Without a word I turn from her and go to my desk, pull open a drawer and take out the box I had in there for safekeeping. Then I turn back to her. She's watching me, still fierce, her posture tense as if she's expecting me to keep fighting.

But I'm not. I'm done. My little *gattina* has won.

Keeping my gaze pinned to hers, I go down on one knee and hold up the box. 'Caterina Salvatore,' I say formally. 'Will you do me the honour of being my wife?'

Shock flickers over her face. 'What do you mean?'

'I'm tired, *gattina.* I'm tired of fighting, tired of pretending. I'm tired of trying to escape the shadow my father cast and I'm tired of being afraid.'

Her eyes widen. 'Vincenzo…'

'I'm afraid I'm not worthy of you, Caterina,' I say, suddenly as fierce as she is. 'But I want to be. And I realise that you're right, I'm *not* Stefano, and I know

I'm not him, because he didn't know what love is. But I do. Because you showed me.'

She swallows, staring at me and I see the tears that fill her eyes.

I rise to my feet, open the box and take out the emerald rings that are still in there. The rings that were always meant for her. And I take her hand and slide them one by one onto her finger. 'I love you,' I say quietly. 'Be my wife. Stay with me. Don't ever leave me.'

She doesn't speak, giving me her answer as she goes up on her toes and presses her mouth to mine.

This time when I reach for her, I don't let her go.

And I never will again.

EPILOGUE

Caterina

I SIT ON a blanket in the shade of the great oak tree that holds court on the rolling lawns of our estate, watching as Vincenzo picks up our three-year-old son, Nico, and tosses him into the air. He's getting too big for these games, but Nico loves it and so does my husband, who indulges him every moment he can get.

I'm holding our new daughter, Elena, who is gazing up at me with her father's big silver eyes. She already has him wrapped around her tiny finger, which is exactly as it should be.

It's been five years since we left Sicily. Vincenzo and I brought the families to heel and made them agree to a truce. Then we did some succession planning. We both wanted to get away from the never-ending arguments and petty disagreements of the families, go somewhere safe to raise children together. But Vincenzo needed to be sure that the Argenti legacy he fought for would remain, and so he called the wider Argenti family to a meeting, informing them that while he would remain as head of the family, he would need someone to act for him in Italy.

He found someone—a distant cousin—who will act on his behalf, while he keeps an eye on the Argentis from a distance. We now live in England, in a beautiful country estate in the Cotswolds, which suits us perfectly.

Vincenzo arranged himself a new identity to protect us from any unwanted family attention and now goes by the name of Vincent Castle. I call him Vinny, just to annoy him.

My Wolf comes over to where I'm sitting with our son tucked under his arm. He puts Nico down and then sits beside me, looking down at our daughter, his silver eyes alight with love.

'I had a thought,' he says, reaching down to touch Elena's cheek with a gentle finger.

'Just the one?' I ask, teasing him.

'Naughty, *gattina,*' he says. 'No, I'm being serious. I've decided that the Argenti legacy was never about stopping the violence, or at least, not entirely.'

'Oh?'

He smiles and my heart skips a beat the way it always does when I look at him. 'No, the true Argenti legacy was always supposed to be love.'

I look at him and our children, and I know that of course my wolf is right. He was always right.

The true Argenti legacy is love and it starts with us.

* * * * *

Keep reading for an excerpt of a new title
from the Romantic Suspense series,
COLTON'S PRIVATE SECURITY by Lisa Childs

Prologue

"Cassidy Garner, RN, report to the ER. Cassidy Garner to the ER ASAP."

The message coming over the PA system at Baldwin Memorial Hospital startled Cassidy. She already had her bag over her shoulder and was heading through the plant-filled atrium of the hospital toward the exit. She was supposed to be done for the night.

But she knew she wouldn't have been paged if it wasn't important. Or…

Something that required her security clearance. "Fern!" Fear rushed up, choking her, as she turned around and ran toward the emergency department.

Not Fern. Please don't let it be Fern.

Cassidy's favorite patient had already been through too much after surviving a harrowing abduction by human traffickers who'd kept her in captivity. When firefighter Ryan Colton rescued Fern, she was brought to Baldwin Memorial to recover from a severely broken leg and other injuries she'd suffered during captivity. Cassidy had been her nurse in a private ward until Fern's release.

She'd been doing so well. Cassidy had just gone by Ryan's place not long ago and caught up with her. Fern wasn't just her former patient; she was going to be a lifelong friend.

Tears stung Cassidy's blue eyes, but she furiously blinked them away. A registered nurse for seven years, she was always professional if not exactly detached. She rolled a hairband off her wrist and bound her blond hair up in it as she neared the doors to the ER. Then she drew in a deep breath, bracing herself, before stepping through them. "I'm here!"

"Cassidy!" Dr. Finkbeiner shouted as she entered. "I need your help!"

She sucked in a breath, worried that the attending physician might have had her paged for another reason that had nothing to do with her nursing skills. "I'm not an ER nurse," she reminded him.

"You've done rotations in the ER a lot."

That was how she'd met him when he'd been a resident, but that was at another hospital where she'd done a stint as a traveling nurse. For four years she'd worked as one before coming back to Dark Canyon, Utah, three years ago.

He gestured at a police officer who stood outside one of the ER bays. "And you're the nurse with the security clearance the police require. C'mon, I need help." He jerked aside the heavy vinyl curtain behind the police officer and stepped into the ER bay.

Cassidy followed him. "What do you need?"

"Another set of hands," he said. "Patient has a lot of contusions, cuts and fractures as well as a possible TBI." Traumatic brain injury.

There was blood everywhere.

"What happened?" she asked as she moved to the other side of the gurney from the doctor and studied the long, lanky man lying on it.

"Automobile crash victim," Finkbeiner replied. "Passenger didn't survive."

"And why the police?" Had he been drinking?

"This guy and the one who died are the human traffickers who abducted that woman who escaped some time ago. But it doesn't matter who he is or what he did, we have to help him." Just as he said it, an alarm went off. "Damn, his heart stopped again! Hurry up!"

Cassidy jumped in to help with CPR. She often rotated through different departments in the hospital, so she was able to tune out everything but her training and her instincts. She put aside her fear and revulsion and anger while they worked on the patient. They got him back, his heart rhythm fast but strong. Then they worked on his other injuries. Once the bleeding was stopped, Cassidy had to wheel the patient off for an MRI to check for internal injuries and that possible TBI.

He hadn't regained consciousness since being brought into the ER, so she shouldn't have been afraid of him. But she couldn't forget that this man had hurt Fern, her friend. He'd been apprehended now, though. And the police officer followed close behind her as she wheeled the gurney to the elevator. Even though the patient was unconscious, the officer was intent on making sure that the criminal did not escape. This man would not hurt Fern again.

But still she felt uneasy as she stepped into the elevator with the gurney and with the officer. "I'm Cassidy," she said and waited for the man to introduce himself.

He just nodded.

The officer looked familiar to her, but maybe that was just because he looked so average. Average build, average height. Light brown hair, light brown eyes, but still…

With everything that had been happening in Dark Canyon lately, there had been a lot of police officers in and out of Baldwin Memorial.

"And you are?" she prodded him.

"Officer Olsen."

She nodded. "That's right. I think we've met before."

He shrugged.

"So what happened tonight?" she asked.

He tensed. "I can't tell you."

"I have security clearance," she reminded him. "That was why I was paged for this patient." Because she'd been cleared to treat the other one: Fern, who'd needed protection from the man on the gurney, and whoever he worked for. Who did he work for? Who in Dark Canyon was behind this horrific human trafficking?

He nodded. "This creep and his buddy abducted that woman again and left her for dead in the fire."

She gasped. "Oh, no! Not Fern." She pressed her hand to her madly pounding heart.

"She survived, with the help of the firefighter she's living with," Olsen assured him. "They're on their way to the hospital now for treatment."

"So they're injured too?" she asked with alarm. And she was torn between treating this patient and making sure that her friend was all right.

He shrugged. "Not seriously. I think just smoke inhalation. The firefighter found her pretty quickly. I guess his bodyguard cousin had some tracking device on her or something."

"Bodyguard cousin?" She tensed as her heart began to beat even harder than it had already been. It couldn't be… No, not Mark. Mark wasn't a bodyguard.

"Yeah, he's some former military guy." He shrugged again as if unconcerned.

But Cassidy was very concerned. Former military. So he had to be talking about Mark Colton. She shouldn't have been surprised because she had recently heard that he was back in Dark Canyon. She did not want to see Mark Colton ever again. Fortunately she hadn't run into him whenever she'd visited Fern at his cousin's place. But her heart pounded madly over how close she must have come to seeing him there since he'd helped his cousin protect Fern. Why was he back in Dark Canyon? Just to see his family? Hopefully Mark would leave again soon, like he always had, still the nomad he'd wanted to be. That she'd once wanted to be, but she'd had to come home three years ago. And she couldn't take off again like he did. She had too many responsibilities, too many people she loved who depended on her, while she had learned, from Mark, to never depend on anyone.

"These Coltons…" the officer murmured and shook his head. "Jacob Colton is the reason this guy is here. He and his team caused the crash."

"Jacob stopped a criminal from escaping justice," she said with some measure of censure. That was a good thing. And Mark, with his tracking device, had made sure that Fern was found. The Coltons were heroes. But this officer didn't seem to think so. And Cassidy wasn't sure why.

But then she couldn't think of Mark as a hero either. She could think of him only as the man who'd broken her heart.

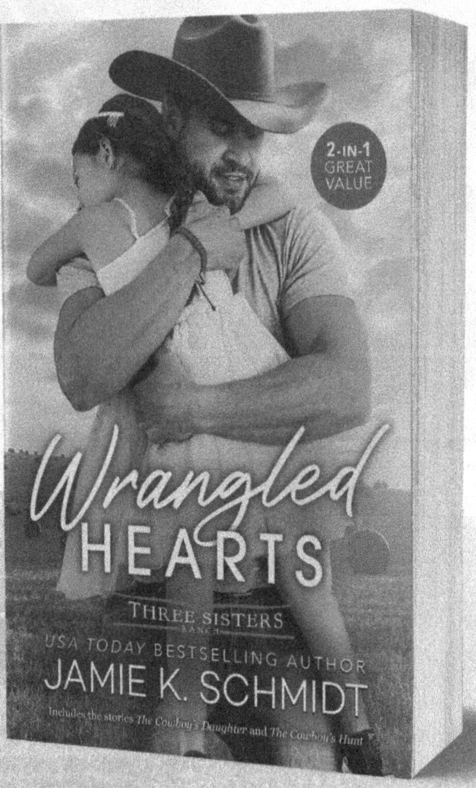
2-IN-1
GREAT
VALUE
Wrangled
HEARTS
THREE SISTERS
RANCH
USA TODAY BESTSELLING AUTHOR
JAMIE K. SCHMIDT
Includes the stories The Cowboy's Daughter and The Cowboy's Hunt